This book is for Hadley and Harper.

I'd also like to thank my publisher and editor Lee D. Thompson for always encouraging me to take chances.

ANIMALS

Jerrod
Edson

First Galleon Edition, August 2025
ISBN 978-1-998122-21-9

Published by Galleon Books
Moncton, New Brunswick, Canada
www.galleonbooks.ca

This is a work of fiction, thank god.

Library and Archives Canada Cataloguing in Publication

Title: Animals / Jerron Edson.
Names: Edson, Jerrod, 1974- author.
Identifiers: Canadiana 20250267438 | ISBN 9781998122219
(softcover)
Subjects: LCGFT: Novellas.
Classification: LCC PS8559.D76 A82 2025 | DDC
C813/.54—dc23

GALLEON

PART 1

$$-1-$$

"9-1-1, what's your emergency?"

"There's someone in my house," she whispers into the phone.

"What's your address, ma'am?"

"18 Baseline Road. I don't know the postal code."

"Ma'am?"

"I just got here today from Ontario."

"I've got it, ma'am, don't worry. Eighteen... One-eight?"

"Yes."

"Baseline Road—"

"Yes."

"Are you alone?"

"My babies," she says. "They're safe. They know where to go."

"Babies?

"My kids."

"How many kids, ma'am?"

"Two—a boy and a girl."

"How old are they?"

"Six and ten."

"They're with you now?"

"No. They got out of the house."

"To be clear, ma'am: They're outside the house?"

She sits up and looks out the window and can see, in the blue of the moonlight, the thin, newly broken trail in the hay leading down the field to the edge of the forest.

"Yes. They're safe. My oldest, Timothy—he knows where to go."

"Are you sure, ma'am?"

"I'm sure."

"Your name, ma'am?'

"Kate Welsh."

There is a moment of silence, only a moment, but it feels much longer.

"It's my husband," she whispers.

"Your husband?"

"Yes. He's crazy. He's an animal."

"What's his name?"

"Anthony Black—*Tony* Black." She can hear the operator typing. "We came here to get away from him. I don't know how he found us so quick."

"Will he harm the children?"

"He's capable of anything. But they're safe now. They know where to go."

"Where are you now, Kate?"

"In my bedroom—by the bed."

"Is the bedroom on the ground floor?"

"Upstairs."

"Is there a closet in the room?"

"Yes."

"I want you to get in it, Kate. Get in the closet right now."

She moves quickly and quietly across the room and into the closet, where there is the bleachy smell from when she'd cleaned it that afternoon, and she remembers how good it had felt when she'd cleaned it; the dust and the dirt along the closet floor wiped clean; how pleased she'd felt when it was finally clean and she'd hung her few clothes and felt that yes, it was a new beginning and this could work here for her and the kids. But the bleachy smell also reminds her that she'd been safe then, those few short hours ago, and for a quick instant she wishes she can step back in time to the safety of the afternoon, but it is only a flash in her mind and now that it is gone, she is more afraid than she'd been a few seconds earlier, before she'd gone into the closet.

Her back rests against the wall, the soft fabric of the hanging dress tickling her nose—the only dress she'd packed—and the thinness of the fabric, the softness of it an absurd and desperate thing, a farce, thinking for a moment it served as some layer of protection.

"Are the police coming? Oh god, please hurry—I don't want to die."

"Kate, listen to me very carefully: I need you to stay calm. The police are on their way."

"Please hurry."

"Breathe, Kate."

She takes a deep, shaky breath.

"Stay where you are, Kate. And stay calm."

"We got away," she continues. "How did he know we were here?"

"Breathe, Kate. Help is coming. Are you sure it's your husband?"

"I don't know," Kate says. "Just please help me. Please!"

...

The farm in Cornhill was Kate's childhood home, and she now owned the property. She'd driven from Mississauga with her two children, the hatchback stuffed full with toys and blankets and clothes, and inside the car the air was stale and smelled of fast food, of hamburgers and fries, but the country breeze in Cornhill was fresh and clean and whooshed it out the window. They'd stopped at Pine Grove Cemetery to see the graves of her parents; her father's headstone with deer and trout, her mother's with flowers.

"Did Grampy like deers?" Timothy asked.

"He did," Kate said.

"Did he have them as pets?"

"No. He was a hunter."

"He killed them?"

"He hunted them."

"So he killed them," Timothy said.

"Hunting and killing isn't the same thing," Kate said.

"What do you mean?"

"I don't know, exactly. I'm not a hunter. It just isn't."

"That doesn't make sense," Timothy said.

"Sometimes things we don't understand don't always make sense to us," Kate said. "But they do to others—and that's OK—we don't need to understand everything in the world."

"What pets did he have?" the girl, Ruby, asked.

Kate sat, legs crossed, on the grass. The children sat on each side of her, picking at the grass.

"Well, he had cows and pigs and chickens."

"Did he kill them?" Timothy asked.

"He was a farmer," Kate said.

"So he hunted them?"

"He was a farmer," Kate said again. "He raised animals for food—not for fun."

"I'm really confused," Timothy said.

"Horses?" Ruby asked.

"He had one horse."

"Did he kill that too?" Timothy asked.

"No."

"What was its name?"

"Murphy."

"*Murphy*?" Ruby said. "Like Murphy's Ice Cream?"

"Yes," Kate said, saddened that she was here now, running, when this time of year they should be back home in Streetsville, sitting at a table in the square, outside of Murphy's, eating ice cream.

Kate looked over to the forest behind the cemetery and could see, with her careful eye, the remnants of fallen trees from a tornado that had swept through Cornhill when she was a girl. Had she not been looking for those fallen trees she wouldn't have seen them. She remembered that day well; her father rushing out to the field, whistling and waving his arms to get the cows into the barn. Her mother told her to get into the cellar below the kitchen. The cellar was dark and cold. Firewood was piled up to the ceiling. She still remembered how cold the stone foundation was against her body as she stood in the darkness, the wind howling outside. It was the only time she'd been that deep in the cellar, behind the woodpile. She was Timothy's age then and she realized Timothy was now more mature, more grown-up than she was at that age, and she knew that if they were going to survive this, that she needed Timothy just as much as Timothy needed her.

Running was the hardest and scariest thing she'd ever done. She knew it would not be easy, but she hadn't expected Timothy to grow up so quickly, literally overnight it seemed. Timothy pulled a handful of grass and tossed it into the air.

"Did you ride him a lot?"

"Who?"

"Murphy."

"Yes," she said. "Almost every day, around the field — not in the hay, but around the outside. At the far corner of the field there were rusted out cars and Murphy and I would go there and I'd climb in the cars and play. He was a lovely horse."

"Can we see the cars? Are they still there?" Timothy asked.

"We can see them, sure."

"Today?"

"Maybe not today," Kate said.

"I want to see the house."

"OK," Kate said, lifting herself from off the grass.

Cornhill was not like Mississauga at all; there were rolling hills and open fields and farms set far off the road, trees lining long, dirt driveways. There were no big buildings, no traffic, no noise. Just the open landscape, the fresh air, the sunshine, and the wide-open blue sky.

"Is this what Mississauga looked like a hundred years ago?" Timothy asked.

Kate laughed.

"Maybe."

"I like it."

"Me too."

Timothy breathed in the fresh air.

"Are we going to live here forever?"

"Forever is a long time," Kate said. "Let's just see how it goes."

"I hope I like it," Ruby said.

"I'm sure you will. It's a special place."

"What's special about it?"

"You'll see."

They pulled into the driveway, which was overgrown with grass. The house was old and looked like it had not been lived in for a very long time, the paint chipping away, cobwebs in the windows, birds' nests tucked up under the ledge on the front porch.

The big barn leaned a little, and there were holes in the tin roof, and holes in the walls where the wood had rotted away. A small chicken coop had collapsed as though it had been shelled. The pigpen stood on the other side of the barn, its wooden shingles weathered.

Stretching three hundred yards behind the barn was a hay field which shone gold in the sun and sloped down to the forest.

"Follow me," Kate said. "I want to show you something before we see the house."

She led them behind the barn, dipping under the wire fence and into the field, pushing the hay aside and running her hands along the soft, fluffy tops of the hay. The field was sloped toward the tree line, followed by the dark of the woods rising into the hilled forest beyond.

"Does he know where we are?" Timothy asked. *He* did not have to be mentioned by name. *He. Him.* The bad man. Their father.

"No," Kate said.

"Will he find us?"

"No."

"I don't want him to ever find us."

"Don't you worry," Kate said. "He doesn't know about this place. Grammy and Grampy died a long time ago and Mommy never told him about it."

"Did you know he was bad when you married him?"

This was a very adult question, and Kate answered it without a filter.

"A small piece of me, perhaps."

Timothy stumbled in the hay and picked himself up.

"Where are we going?"

"You'll see."

They came to the clearing at the end of the field that separated the field from the forest.

"The cars are over there," she pointed.

She led them to the tree line, toward a fallen tree so big and grey it looked like the fossil of some prehistoric beast. Kate walked them around the tree and there, pulling away some weeds and brush, was a burrow between the trunk and the ground. Kate got on her hands and knees and crawled inside. It was damp and dirty and dark under the tree and Kate had to crouch low, her face near her knees as she huddled with them. It was a smaller space than she remembered, but big enough for the three of them. She turned on her phone light and set it at her feet.

"This is where you come if there is danger," she said. "Do you think you can find it on your own?"

"I think so," Timothy said.

"Just get across the field and if you come out at a different place, walk along the edge of the trees and you'll find it. You can't miss it. Even in the dark the moon will light it up."

Ruby dug her fingers into the dirt.

"I like it here."

"I like it too," Timothy said, bumping his head on a root and knocking some dirt into his hair.

"It's our secret," Kate said.

"Like the Secret Garden," Ruby said.

"Yes," Kate said. "Maybe we can get some snacks and have them here in case you need them."

"Do you think we'll need them, Mom?" Timothy asked.

Kate was sad and relieved that Timothy was old enough to understand how important this was.

"I don't know," she said. "But if the time comes you bring Ruby here and you stay here until I come get you. No matter what, you stay here. Do you understand?"

Timothy nodded.

"Can we get some juice boxes?"

Kate smiled.

"Of course. Anything you want."

"I want a fruit roll," Ruby said. "And Bear Paws and licorice."

"Why is Dad like that?" Timothy asked.

"He just is," Kate said.

"He's bad, isn't he?"

"He is."

"Will I be bad like him? Jenny said we grow up just like our parents."

Kate smiled sadly. "You're nothing like him."

"Can we get granola bars too?" Ruby asked. She was making a small pile out of the loose earth between her feet, sweeping it together with her hands.

They crawled out of the burrow and back into the light.

"You can see the tip of the barn from here if you get up on your tippy-toes," Kate said. "But you don't come out unless I come. Do you understand?"

Timothy rolled his eyes.

Kate took him by the arms.

"I mean it, Timothy. I need you to be a big boy and tell me you understand."

Timothy looked his mother in the eyes.

"I got it, Mom."

Kate sighed.

"Good."

A branch snapped not too far away, in the bushes, and Timothy jumped.

"What was that?"

Kate smiled.

"It's just an animal," she said. "We're in the woods. There are animals in the woods. This isn't Streetsville. Now let's go see the house, shall we?"

...

They were sweaty by the time they crossed the courtyard and into the old house. The door was unlocked, passing through the front porch and stepping into the kitchen. The floor and counters were covered with a layer of dust, and there were cobwebs and flies and a quiet to the house that made everything they did seem louder than it was.

The floor creaked underfoot, the ripple of disturbing its slumber.

"Is this house haunted?" Ruby asked, holding Kate's hand.

Kate smiled. "No. Nobody has been here in a while. That's all." She sighed heavily. "We've got some work to do."

Timothy swept his foot along the dusty floor.

"I think we need a shovel."

...

Kate's head is buried between her knees, the hanging dress tickling the top of her head, the phone pressed to her ear.

"Is your bedroom door locked?" the operator asks.

"Oh my god, no—"

She drops the phone and slides the closet door open.

"Kate, stay where you are…Kate?"

The phone is on the floor and she is out of the closet, feeling exposed as she moves quickly across the room, toward the door. She hears mumbled voices at the top of the stairs as she clicks the lock on the door then skips back to the closet and slides the door shut and picks up the phone again.

"Kate?"

"I'm here," she whispers, more quietly now, her breath louder than her voice.

"Kate, I need you to stay in the closet, and stay on the phone with me. Do you understand?"

"They're upstairs."

"What side of the house is the bedroom—north, south?"

"I don't know," she says. "It's at the end of the hall."

"Are you the only one in the house now?"

"Yes—where are the police?"

"They're on their way. But for now I'm going to need you to be brave."

"OK," she whispers. She is shaking. "I shouldn't be talking."

"Can you still hear them?"

She cups her hand around her mouth, covering the phone.

"Yes."

"Stay where you are."

There is a long pause. The operator listens to Kate breathing into the phone.

Kate's breathing quickens.

"They're in the hall."

"OK," the operator says. "Don't talk. Just breathe."

— 2 —

"9-1-1, what's your emergency?"

"I've been shot," he says, gasping. He can taste the blood in his mouth and spits it out. He is sitting against a pine tree.

"What's your location, sir?"

"I'm in the woods behind my house on Meenan's Cove Road—Gondola Point."

"What number house, sir?"

"Seventeen."

"One-seven?"

"Yes."

"Are you able to move, sir?"

He grunts. "I've got an arrow in my side."

"An arrow, sir?"

"An arrow. I'm being hunted."

"Repeat that again, please, sir?"

"I'm being hunted," he says.

"Sir, are you able to give me your exact location?"

He cringes and grunts.

"I'm in the woods behind my house. Please hurry. They're coming."

"Who, sir? Who is coming?"

"Whoever is hunting me."

The pain strikes his side again. It feels like lightning. He digs his fingers into the loose earth around him until the pain passes and for a moment he looks up at the sun coming through the trees.

"Do you have a GPS locator on your phone, sir?"

"I'm an old man," he says. "I don't know what that is."

"What kind of phone do you have, sir?"

"They're coming," he says. "I need to move or I'm dead."

"Move then, quickly," the operator says.

Below him, he sees the row of trees along the path with the tin cans sharply reflecting in the sun. He does not think of his trail of blood on the ground. Nor does he see the hunters moving swiftly and quietly toward him. He knows these woods like he knows his own street, but he has never been this far up the hillside.

"Can I get your name, sir?"

"Mel Tinsel."

"T-I-N—" the operator says, typing.

"S-E-L," the old man says. He grunts again. The arrow sticks out from his ribs. "I'm the Tin Man."

"Repeat, sir?"

"The Tin Man," he says. "There was a story on me in the *Telegraph-Journal*."

"Sir, I'm not aware of that."

"The trees," he says, looking down on them. "People know of them. They know where they are."

"Police are on their way, sir. Stay where you are."

"Tell them to go to the Tin Man's trees."

"Sir?"

"They'll know," he says.

"The Tin Man's trees," the operator says. "OK."

"I can see them," the old man says, spotting the moving figures making their way across the clearing. It is odd seeing things from so high up; he'd never seen his trees from this angle and they look so beautiful from up here, how they sparkle along the path that curves and snakes through the woods. He grunts again, then spits another mouthful of blood.

…

Mel Tinsel had always enjoyed walks in the woods behind his house. He loved sitting on a stump with his thermos full of hot tea and listening to everything around him. He was a man who understood nature and understood the language of the forest, the rustle of leaves high in the wind and the birds singing within them.

His wife had died ten years before. Together they raised two boys, Steven and Bill, who had long since moved out and called most weekends but rarely visited. They didn't live very far away, but Mel had always felt as though he were intruding whenever he went to see them. Steven managed the family business, Mel's Shoe Emporium. Bill taught Math at a high school in Sussex. And so Mel found other things to pass the time, like playing chess against himself or solving a puzzle or reading a good book. But most of all he enjoyed walking through the woods with his .22, pretending to shoot at birds, though never actually doing it.

On his way back home one summer afternoon he picked up an old tin can that was half-buried in the ground. He placed it on a branch, counted twenty paces and took aim. As he eyed his target through the sight he noticed that a flicker of sunlight had broken through the trees and sparkled in the can. And suddenly he felt the way he did when aiming at a bird and he couldn't pull the trigger. He lowered the rifle and took a step back. The sparkling can reminded him of a Christmas tree ornament, which made him think of his boys and of his late wife.

Every Christmas when the boys were young, Mel would wake up early and hide behind the couch to tape them tiptoeing out to the tree in their pajamas to see what Santa had brought. The camera had a bright light and it reflected off the ornaments, and now, staring at the dirty tin can on the branch, Mel's heart fluttered when he realized how long ago those days had been—how far away they'd become.

When he got home he went straight to the attic, found the box of film and loaded it into the camera. And there his family was on the screen; his boys were boys again, his wife played with her hair the way she always did when he filmed her. She had thick blonde hair back in those days and she would curl it in her fingers while pretending not to be flustered by the camera. She would often look into it and tell Mel to shut it off.

"I'm serious, Mel," she would say.

"It's not recording."

"I can see the little red light."

"Tell me you love me."

She would smile back.

"I love you. Now turn it off."

Mel sat in the attic and watched every roll of film in the box. The next day he went to the cupboard and emptied every soup can into the sink. Then he went to the garage for the cans he had saved for minor hockey. He called the grocery store and bought a dozen flats of canned beans and emptied them all. He drilled holes in each can and tied a string through each hole. By noon he was back in the woods, looking for the tree with the old can on the branch. When he found it he hung all the cans on the tree then took twenty paces back and looked at them in the sunlight. Then he sat down and stared, and it wasn't long before he drifted off to a time when life was good, when everything sparkled around the Christmas tree and he'd hid behind the couch, looking through the camera. His two boys came downstairs in their pajamas.

"Holy cow!" Bill gasped when he saw the Big Wheels parked in front of the tree.

"Look!" Steven said, pointing to the Hot Wheels racetrack that was set up on the living room floor.

"Holy shit!" Bill said.

Mel tried not to laugh when Bill spotted the camera and realized his father had heard him curse.

"Take down your socks," Mel said, camera still running. "See what else Santa brought."

The old man walked home from the woods that night, saddened yet again that it was all such a long time ago.

The next morning he called the grocery store. This time he bought a thousand cans—soup, tuna, dog food—whatever they had. It took him two days, first emptying them in the backyard, peeling off labels, then drilling and tying the string. It took him three days to decorate ten more trees. But it was worth it. He spent every day lying on his back in the middle of the woods, the cold earth below him, the cans swaying in the trees. And now, with eleven trees surrounding him, he was not only able to dream about Christmas, but of any day he wished. It was then that Mel decided to decorate all the trees along the path. He called the recycling plant in the city and had a dump truck deliver the load.

It took him three months to decorate the trees. And every morning Mel awoke and went into the woods to dream. Somehow the newspaper heard of it, and a reporter had come to his house and Mel took him into the woods and showed him. The story was in the paper a few days later.

...

Mel is slouched, and he props himself up against the tree, feeling the cool breeze along the hill, and he shivers.

"I've lost a lot of blood."

"I need you to stay strong," the operator says.

Mel cringes and smiles at the same time.

"Young man, I'm dying."

"Don't give up on me," the operator says.

Mel cringes again but doesn't smile.

"I'm not giving up. But I know if I don't get to a hospital soon I'm a goner."

There is a moment of silence. It seems that calling the operator 'young man' has sucked some of the operator's confidence.

"Help is on the way."

"I need you to do something for me," Mel says.

"Sir?"

"This conversation is recorded, is it not?"

"It is, sir."

Mel grunts and shivers.

"Then let my boys hear this."

"Sir?"

"Steven, look after your brother. You know what I mean. Keep him close. Invite him to dinner. Let him see his nieces." He grunts again and coughs up a clump of blood and wipes his mouth on his sleeve. "Bill. Don't worry so much. Life is good. Enjoy it. Enjoy every moment of it."

"Sir, I—"

"Call me Mel."

"Mel," the operator says. "You can do this. You're not going to die."

Mel manages a grin.

"I appreciate that, son. I really do."

"Sir. Mel—"

"I'm not giving up just yet," Mel says. "Don't you worry." He lifts himself to his feet, leans against the tree. The figures move through the trees below, climbing. His ribs burn, really burn, like they're on fire, stinging and burning and he presses against them, fighting it, trying to push the burn back into his body. Blood is down his pantleg and his pants are stuck to his skin. He knows he needs to move, and before he does, he takes one last look down at his trees.

...

Often while under the sparkling trees, Mel returned to the times he and his wife took the boys camping in PEI. The ferry ride was especially fun, the boys wide-eyed down where the cars were parked, the waves crashing up against the side of the boat, and then, when they climbed the stairs to the deck, a wide blue sky, a cool and salty summer breeze, and the island blurry in the distance. His wife wore big sunglasses and a red and white striped sweater that made her look like Jackie O. The boys hung their arms over the railing and looked out to the cold black of the water and the white scratches of breaks and waves.

"Are there sharks in there, Dad?"

"Of course."

"Big ones?"

"Huge—like Jaws."

They would drive to the other side of the island, to Cavendish, where they stayed at a campground near the ocean. They walked through a hay field to get to the beach. The boys used to hide in the hay and Mel and his wife would try to find them and they would laugh and scream and wrestle him down. They took pictures of only their heads sticking out of the hay, and at night they would roast marshmallows on a campfire. Mel's wife always burned hers but she would eat them anyway, saying she liked it that way. Mel would concentrate and brown one perfectly and then give it to her and watch her enjoy it for real.

Sometimes when Mel woke up under the trees he would see the cans and think, briefly, that he had died and was with his wife in heaven. Then he would pick himself up from off the ground and make his way back to his quiet house.

One afternoon he dreamt of Halloween when his boy Steven was seven and had insisted on being Wonder Woman. He was dressed in his mother's red leotards, a brown bra and a long black wig. When Mel tried to tell him that he couldn't dress as Wonder Woman the boy got upset.

"Why not?"

"Because she's a woman. How about Batman?"

"I don't like Batman."

"Superman?"

Mel's wife took a picture of Steven with the leotards pulled up over his belly, and the bra that hung down to his waist. She told Steven it was a wonderful costume and out he went.

...

The hillside is steeper now as Mel climbs, reaching for roots and trees, moving as fast as he can. The earth gives way under his feet and he falls onto his side, snapping the arrow in two, and he shrieks and drops the phone and reaches for it.

"Are you there?" he grunts.

"I'm here, sir — Mel," the operator says.

"I'm moving up the hillside. I'm circling around. I'll need to get over the hill and come down the other side. It'll bring me back to Meenan's Cove Road."

"What is your condition, sir?"

He looks down at his side, at the broken arrow protruding from his ribs. His shirt is sticky with blood.

"I don't know if I'll make it." He gasps, sharply, the pain worse now that he'd seen all the blood. He hears sirens in the distance. Or does he? His ears are ringing. There is a long way to go, and he keeps climbing, the sweat and blood and dirt leaving a trail behind him as he claws his way up to the top of the ridge. From here he can see the ferry to Kingston Peninsula, and the stretch of the Kennebecasis River, all the way to the big Tudor house where the river bends, and all the green hills on Kingston and beyond, the blue of the sky and the few small clouds high up. There is no more beautiful place to die, he thinks, then he breathes and grunts and keeps going. They are behind him and if they are good hunters they will track him easily. He can see, far below, Meenan's Cove Road winding through the trees. A car passes along the road in silence.

—3—

"9-1-1, what's your emergency?"

"There's someone in the building with a gun," he says. He is crouched under his desk, in his cubicle. His plump body is bent round, his khakis stretched tight at the thighs, the back of his head pressed against the underside of his desk. He leans as far forward as he can to grab the leg of his chair and slide it toward him.

"What's your address, sir?"

"2 Robert Speck Parkway," he says. "I'm on the tenth floor."

He listens and hears nothing, and he regrets not running out with everyone else. But when he'd heard the gunshots and the screams his first instinct had been to duck and hide, and that's what he'd done. But now he is trapped.

"How many people are with you, sir?"

"I don't know."

"Sir?"

"I don't know," he says again. "It's a huge room with cubicles. Everyone ran out when they heard the shots. I don't know if anyone else is here. Should I call out for them?"

"No. Stay where you are," the operator says.

His back is beginning to cramp and he tries to adjust himself, inch by inch, sliding his legs so that his belly is squished between them. He feels the crotch of his khakis give way, and the tear sounds louder than it is, but with the crotch torn the tightness releases from his thighs.

"I'm in the far corner under my desk," he says. "I haven't heard any shots since the first ones. Maybe it was a false alarm."

"It is not," the operator says. "Police are on their way. Stay where you are. Can I have your name, sir?"

"Terry Buckman," he says.

"Ok, Terry, we'll get you through this."

"I don't want to die," he says. "This is the best job I've ever had."

...

Terry Buckman had always been a shy, quiet, obese kid. And because he was shy and quiet and obese, no one ever paid him any attention. And so he occupied himself with books and movies and video games, and his part-time job stocking shelves at Longo's grocery store on Thomas Street in Mississauga. It was there, at Longo's, that he made friends — not friends he hung out with outside of work, but friends he was able to talk to, and who talked to him, and they joked and laughed, and Terry, for the first time in his life, felt a part of something. In high school he worked every Friday and Saturday night, but in the summers he worked five nights a week, and in his graduation year he stayed on in September.

The cereal skids were the best. They were the biggest and the lightest and he could go through them quickly. His manager, Dan, would grin when Terry cleared the first skid in a matter of minutes.

"You're a hell of a worker, Terry. But don't kill yourself. Take your time. We've got all night." He leaned in close. "Just between me and you, I wish I had more workers like you." Then he winked and smiled.

Later that year, Terry was named assistant supervisor of the night crew, a title he was very proud of. The workers liked him, and the more confident he became, the more his personality shone; he was quick-witted, and charming. The running joke was that the cereal skid was always his, and had he been given a skid of soup or apples, Terry never would have been named assistant supervisor. This was not a hidden joke, or something with malice, and Terry too often referred to himself as Captain Crunch for the cereal skid.

Then there was Lisa.

Lisa from the bakery.

She was awkwardly skinny, bony, flat chested, and had tiny blemishes on her forehead. But she was pretty, with big green eyes and short brown hair and freckles along her nose that made Terry sweat a little whenever he spoke to her. She always wore a flower clip flattening her short bangs, and with her freckles it made her look like a pixie. The crew often joked that when standing side by side Terry and Lisa looked like the number 10. Terry would laugh it off, but inside it just made him sweat more.

The bakery crew arrived at 5:00 each morning. Terry tried to be by the front doors around that time. It was easy; he saved the water skids for then. And he would always glance out the big front windows to the empty parking lot to see Lisa's car pull in.

"Morning, Terry," she always said.

"Oh, morning, Lisa," Terry would respond. The goal was to strike a conversation but he had no idea how to do it. He would try things like "Hey, cold night out there, eh?" or "Did you see the Leafs last night?" But she would simply smile and answer quickly and keep going. It wasn't until Terry changed his plan and timed it so he was near the bakery that he was able to have actual conversations with her. She liked the same tv shows, and she liked movies. And therein Terry developed his plan to ask her out. The new *Stars Wars* movie was coming out soon. They'd talked of *Star Wars* a few times; he didn't care for the Disney movies but he loved the originals. Lisa, bony arms wrapped behind her skinny frame to tie her apron, would disagree.

"I love the new ones. They're so much fun."

"Yeah, OK, they're fun," Terry said. "But the storylines aren't as good."

Lisa took out her flower clip and stretched the dark netting over her head.

"You're crazy. I can't wait for the next one to come out."

"It's out next week."

"I know."

There was a second or two of silence and Terry could feel sweat forming down the middle of his back.

"So maybe, I was thinking, maybe—"

He was leaning on a skid of pop, and the skid started to lean and he reached over and tried to grab it but it was a heavy skid and, as the cases started to fall, Terry threw his body over the skid and he tumbled over it in a heap. One of the cases broke open and a few bottles of Coke fizzed out onto the floor. As Terry picked himself up, his shirt caught on one of the cases and ripped from the collar to the waist and had swiped off his body as quickly and as smoothly as a magician swipes his cape at the end of a trick. Terry's white belly mushroomed and sagged over his pants, and there he stood.

A few of the crew came over. Terry, his shirt at his feet, torn and wet with Coke, could do nothing but stand there.

One of the younger ones on the crew, Andre, chuckled. "At least it's Diet Coke."

And everyone laughed.

Except for Lisa.

And it was Lisa's not-laughing that hurt Terry. She pitied him. And pity was always worse than humiliation. Their eyes met in a moment of understanding; that he could see that she was pitying him, and she could see that that had hurt him.

"I'm more of a Pepsi girl," she said. And she did her best to laugh at her own joke.

...

Terry's neck begins to ache, and he thinks about Longo's now, and what he would be doing if he'd still worked there. He twists his wrist and checks his watch. It is just before 9:00. He would've been sleeping now, comfortable in his bed after his shift.

"I don't know how much longer I can stay under my desk."

"It is the safest place to be," the operator says.

"Is this a terrorist attack?"

"I don't have that information," the operator says.

"Police are here?"

"They're on their way."

"Then I'm coming out," Terry says. "I can't fit under my desk any longer."

"Stay where you are," the operator says.

Terry, as carefully and quietly as he can, pushes the chair out. Moving the chair makes him feel exposed. But his legs below the knees have pins and needles, and his neck aches, and his back is cramping, and if he doesn't get out from under the desk he is going to faint. He bends round as much as he can, almost to the point where he feels his spine will snap, places his palms flat on the floor, and crawls out. He sits on the floor and looks under his desk and wonders how he'd gotten under there so easily. He doubts he can fit under there again. At eye level, he sees his keyboard, and the small stack of cheques next to it. His monitor is frozen where he'd left it, the tab blinking, ready for input. It is odd, the stillness of everything, as if on display in a museum. The only thing he hears is the hum of the fluorescent lights overhead. He'd never noticed this before. He also notices that his shirt is stuck to him from sweat, and he feels the sweat down his spine and inside his thighs.

"Terry?"

Terry puts the phone to his ear. "I'm out. I couldn't stay under there."

"Terry, I don't recommend this. Police have arrived. They will be in the building shortly. You should get back under the desk where it is safe."

"I think I'm the only one here."

"You're not," the operator says.

"Who else is here?"

"I don't have that information. But there have been other calls from inside the building. Just stay where you are and you're going to get through this."

"It could be Larry."

"Who is that?" the operator asks.

Terry can hear the operator typing.

"Larry Williams," he said. "He was fired last week. He worked two cubicles down from me. He was mad as hell when he left."

"Do you know his address?"

"It's somewhere in Port Credit. By the Go Station."

Terry listened as the operator speaks to another line, informing them of the name Larry or Lawrence Williams.

"How old is Mr. Williams?"

"Around fifty."

"Describe him."

"Tall. Thin. Long grey beard. Smells like cigarettes."

The operator is typing.

"We got along," Terry says. "But what if he's coming after Barb? My cubicle is right beside her office."

"Who is Barb?"

"My manager. She fired Larry. He was yelling at her when he left. They had to get Security to escort him out of the building."

"Terry, you need to get back under your desk. You need to trust me on this."

Terry looks under his desk. "I can't. Maybe I can crawl to another cubicle away from Barb's office."

"Get back under your desk, Terry. Please."

"I can hear the sirens now."

He crawls down the row of cubicles and from the floor it feels like a maze. His knee catches his tie and he lurches forward. He pulls off his tie and tosses it aside and carries on. His knees burn against the carpet. He turns into the next row and heads straight to the back, into a manager's cubicle where he can see out the window and down to the parking lot. Two police cars have just arrived, their lights flashing. The parking lot across the street is filling with people who've gotten out of the building. Terry wishes again that he'd run out with them. He waits a moment. Just the hum of the lights, and he knows he is alone.

"Terry, are you there?"

"I moved."

"Tell me your location."

"I'm one row over, against the windows, in an office."

"Close the office door."

"There's no door. Just a big partition."

"Get under the desk, Terry. Now."

Terry lifts his head and peers over the desk, to the far side of the room. He tucks his head back down and holds the phone close.

"Are they on my floor?"

"I don't know," the operator says. "You are on the tenth floor, Terry, correct?"

"Yes," he says.

"Southwest side."

"Yes," he says again.

...

He'd just finished a skid of pet food when his manager approached. Terry was sweating as usual, working diligently.

"Let's go grab a coffee," his manager said, whose name was Jason, and who was tall and thin and had the same tired eyes all the night crew had.

They walked across the empty parking lot to McDonalds. It was well after midnight and the restaurant was closed, though the drive-thru stayed open all night, and they walked through the drive-thru, got their coffees, then sat on the curb. Jason lit a cigarette. He took a drag and exhaled.

"Nice night," he said.

Terry sipped his coffee. He'd never taken a break so early in his shift before, and never had Jason asked him to have a coffee, and so he knew something was up.

Jason smoked and exhaled heavily.

"Terry, you're a hell of a worker."

"Thanks," Terry said. He sipped his coffee. He could feel it coming.

"Terry," Jason said. "We're making some changes. We gotta cut two from the crew. Budgets and all that shit." He took a drag of his cigarette and a sip of coffee, allowing for a few seconds of uneasy silence. "We gotta cut the two highest paid guys. I'm sorry."

Terry felt a hotness start in his feet and up through his legs.

"I'm fired?"

"Not fired," Jason said. "Laid off."

Again a silence. A car pulled into the lot, the lights glaring in their eyes as it slowed and turned into the drive-thru.

"I don't understand," Terry said.

"You got two weeks," Jason said. He nudged him. "But between you and me, you can leave right now and still get paid."

"I don't want to leave," Terry said. "I'll take less pay."

"Ah shit," Jason said. "Don't sell yourself short." He glanced back at the grocery store, at the big red Longo's sign sending a red glow down onto the empty lot. "Let me tell you something, you don't want to end up like me. Forty years old and working some shit overnight job a high school kid could do. You should consider yourself lucky."

Terry stared down at his feet.

"I don't feel lucky."

"*You*'ll be fine," Jason said. "You know who's not gonna be fine?"

Terry said nothing, letting Jason answer.

"Lisa."

Terry looked up.

"She digs you, man," Jason said. "Shit, you're the only one who doesn't see it."

Terry managed a bit of a grin. "I see it."

Jason laughed.

"Atta boy!"

A police car raced up Thomas Street, lights flashing, but no siren, and they watched as it flew up the street. Then there was the stillness of the parking lot again.

Terry sighed deeply.

"This is the only job I've ever had."

Jason took another drag of his cigarette then flicked it onto the pavement. Both of them watched it smoke and die out.

"There's a recruitment office on Hurontario near the 403. My sister works there. She'll find you a job."

"Your sister? Why don't you get her to get you another job?"

Jason glanced over at the grocery store and grinned.

"And leave all this?"

...

Terry finished his shift that night and never went back. He went to the recruitment office the next day. He filled out a form listing his skills and quickly realized he didn't have very many. He was not good at typing, but he lied, saying he knew Excel and Word and could type sixty words per minute. He was called into an office to discuss his form. Terry was sure it was Jason's sister.

"You've got the same eyes as Jason," he said, sitting snuggly in the chair opposite the desk. It was a small office which made him uncomfortable; he was not used to anything as formal or as confined as this. His shirt collar was tight, and he'd tied his tie too tight, and he began to sweat.

She simply smiled.

"You can type," she said.

He paused.

"Yes."

She tapped a few keys on her keyboard and stared at her screen, which Terry could not see.

"Type fast?" she asked, not looking at him. "Sixty words a minute?"

He did his best to look confident. "Yes. Fast enough."

She tapped at the keyboard.

"I may have something for you. This job is about production. My brother says you're a hard worker."

"I try my best."

She glanced down at the form.

"No criminal record?"

"No."

"When are you available to start?"

"Tomorrow," Terry said. "I didn't expect this to be so easy."

She kept her eyes on the screen.

"Well, you still have to impress your employer. I can only get you in the door."

…

That was six weeks ago.

Terry had worked hard at his new job, inputting student loan cheques into a database, calculating each batch, separating the federal loans from the provincial loans, and how proud he felt having to dress up for work each day, wearing a shirt and tie, and having his own cubicle, and the manager who told him he was doing a fine job.

This was the day he was going to surprise his buddies at Longo's with coffees; he hadn't seen them since he'd left. He was going to be there at midnight, and best of all, he was going to meet Lisa in the parking lot and ask her out. On a date. To see the *Star Wars* movie, which he knew she'd likely already seen by now, but that didn't matter.

"Are you there, Terry?" the operator asks.

"Yes."

"Are you under the desk?"

"No. I can't fit."

"Get under the desk, Terry, please."

"I don't understand this. I don't understand this at all. Why is this happening?"

"Stay calm, Terry."

"I'm going to die, aren't I?"

"You're not going to die. Listen to me, Terry. You're going to be fine. Just get under the desk and stay quiet. You can do this. Say it: I can do this."

Terry is crying.

"I'm going to die. I need to get out of the building. I should've ran out with everyone else. I need to get out!"

"Stay where you are," the operator says.

"I'm getting out of here."

"Terry, please, get under the desk. It is the safest place to be."

Terry pokes his head up over the desk. The room is quiet. Then, slowly, he lifts himself from off the floor and stands up straight. His heart beats against his shirt collar. He takes a long, uneven breath, and looks around the empty room.

PART 2

$$-1-$$

A rusted pickup truck speeds along the winding dirt road, spitting up pebbles and a cloud of dust. It rattles the faster it goes, and there is a toolbox in the back that bounces and slides across the metal. In the cab, behind the seat, a hammer, some loose shotgun shells, various coins, and two rifles rattle and bump with the road.

A rhinoceros is driving.

His hide is thick and wrinkled and tattooed, but the tattoos are faded and they look like veins. The wrinkles on his face are deep and make thick rings around his tiny black eyes. At the end of his snout is a worn horn, yellowed and chipped with age. He chews on an unlit cigar. His arm hangs out the window. The dirt road winds through the trees, in and out of the sunlight, and the old truck speeds along, hitting holes and rocks and dips. The rhino floors it on the straightaways, easing up ever so slightly on the turns, the truck skidding and drifting a little before straightening out again.

Sitting beside the rhino is his friend, the lion.

The lion grips the dashboard. His mane whirls about, whipping across his face and in his eyes as the violent wind in the cab swirls and blows loud in his ears and face.

The rhino, chewing on his cigar, turns to the lion and grins.

"You alright?"

"I'm fine," the lion says, raising his voice above the wind. He swipes at his mane, moving it from his eyes, only to have it sweep across his face again.

The rhino is still grinning.

"You look like you're gonna shit yourself."

The lion looks straight ahead.

"Just watch the road, please."

The rhino laughs and hits the gas.

"You want this, right?"

The lion looks straight ahead and nods.

"You trust me?" the rhino asks.

The lion nods again.

"Good," the rhino says. "You got nothing to worry about. This time next week you'll be sittin' pretty."

The lion grips the dashboard tighter at the upcoming turn.

"If you don't kill us before we get there."

"Ha!" the rhino roars. He spits the cigar out the window and turns to the lion again. "Just remember what you're doing this for."

The lion stiffens as the truck skids around the turn.

"Buck up," the rhino says. "Ain't nothing more good than looking out for your family. You hear me?"

The lion nods.

"You lost your way," the rhino says. "Shit happens. We've known each other how long now?"

"Since we were kids," the lion says, rolling his eyes. He has been asked this question already today.

The rhino horks and spits out the window.

"You're just like a brother to me and brothers pick each other up when they're down." He spits out the window again. "You know what I'm sayin', right?"

"Yes."

"Then why you look like you're gonna shit yourself? You can tell your old man about this. He'd like it."

The lion's father was a hunter, and had tried to pass it down to him, but the lion did not understand it; to him it was senseless. But he knew there was more to it than that; that his suburban self did not understand the code of the hunter and the places of this code within the hidden wonders of the forest. But this, he thought, his mane blowing about in the cab. This I can tell him about, and he'll be proud. Today you're hunting and tomorrow you can tell him all about it. OK, you can do this. He grips the dashboard as the truck skids around another turn.

"Slow down, please!"

The rhino laughs and hits the gas.

...

The lion had once been the proudest of his pride. He'd built a successful business that was listed among the top builders in the region. He could drive through any part of the province and proudly point out a neighbourhood he'd built. There, that one—two hundred dens—an all-lion neighbourhood. And that one. Every bit of it. He also had a successful marriage. Cubs grown and raised and had left the den and had litters of their own.

But business had faltered with the housing crash. The lion's wife had never asked about it and he'd never told her; he let her remain blissful in her ignorance, happy with their lives, their lifestyles.

Little did she know that for the past year they'd been living off credit cards, and within the year, they'd be bankrupt.

On their drive to the rhino's house, the lion's wife, holding a potato salad in her lap, smiled as they pulled onto the rhino's street. It was not a neighbourhood like their own; the lots were small, the houses dated to the seventies, and there were no sidewalks. Indeed, their luxury sedan was noticed as they drove along.

"I hope they like the salad," the lion's wife said. "I put dill in it. Do they eat dill? I don't think they've been over when I've put dill in it."

"It'll be fine," the lion said. "Look at the size of them; they eat anything."

The lion's wife slapped him lightly.

"Be nice," she said. "They're just built that way. They're not like us. They're not cats. And I think it's wonderful how you two have stayed friends for so long, since you were a cub. That's a special thing, to have a friend like that."

"He's a good guy," the lion said.

"He's resourceful too," the lion's wife said.

The lion frowned. "How so?"

"To go from one job to the next. What does he even do now?"

"He's a contractor."

"What does that even mean?"

"It means he's a contractor."

"He doesn't work much, is all I'm saying. Yet he always seems to have money."

The lion grinned. "You got me there," he said. "He's never been one to work much."

The lion felt his wife looked especially pretty today; how she sat, the wind blowing her fur.

There'd been a pit in his stomach since his business troubles began; he'd seen it coming from a distance: less and less builders, fewer new homes, and now, as he looked at his wife, and how pretty she looked, smiling for no reason but that she felt happy sitting there, in their luxury sedan, comfortable, holding the potato salad she'd made herself, the pit in his stomach grew.

"You know," the lion's wife said. "You could offer him a job."

The lion huffed. "Why? Where's this coming from?"

"Oh, I don't know," she said. "Just this neighbourhood. It's not safe. Do you know there were two home invasions last week? I saw it on the news."

"Hyenas, no doubt," the lion said.

"Of course."

"There's lots of them in this area."

As they approached the rhino's house they both saw, at the same time, a luxury sedan like theirs, only a newer model, parked in the driveway, next to the rhino's rusted pickup truck.

"You told me we were the only ones coming over," the lion's wife said, clutching the bowl of potato salad a little tighter.

The lion pulled into the driveway.

The rhino opened his front door, the bulk of his frame filling the doorframe.

"Come on 'round the back," he shouted, then retreated into the house.

The lion and his wife made their way around to the side, where the rhino met them. It was an unkempt backyard, but with a new set of outdoor furniture on the patio, where the rhino's wife sat sipping on a drink.

"Hello!" she said. She and the lion's wife hugged. She took the bowl of potato salad. "Come on inside; we'll put it in the fridge. And you've got to see the new kitchen."

The rhino was smoking a cigar. He leaned down and plucked a can of beer from the cooler and handed it to the lion.

"How do ya like the new wheels?"

The lion peered toward the direction of the driveway.

"That's yours?"

The rhino nodded and chugged down the last of his beer, crushed the can and tossed it at the foot of the barbeque amongst three other crushed cans.

"Did you steal it?" the lion asked.

"Ha!" the rhino roared. "Just picked it up yesterday."

"Not too shabby," the lion said.

Smoke came from the barbeque and the rhino opened the lid and took the tongs and flipped the steaks.

"Smells good," the lion said. He looked down at the meat sizzling on the grill, then sniffed. There was a sweetness coming from the grill, and a thickness to the meat that was noticeable. But it was the sweetness that made it unique; there was only one kind of meat that had that smell; gamy and alluring.

"That's not what I think it is."

The rhino, cigar between his thick leathery lips, grinned.

"Oh, it is."

"Where the hell did you get those?"

"You don't wanna know what I paid for them," the rhino said.

The patio doors slid open and the two wives stepped out and sat at the table. They were chuckling over something.

The lion lowered his voice. He was still looking down at the steaks.

"Where did you get them?" he asked again.

The rhino shrugged. "I know a few hyenas down the way."

"So from what, like a black market?" The lion sipped his beer and waited for a response.

The rhino nodded and sucked on his cigar.

"Yeah, somethin' like that."

"I didn't know those things actually existed."

"There's a black market for everything," the rhino said. "You want skin shoes, there's a market. I can make a call and have skull bowls delivered here today if I want."

"You're shitting me," the lion said.

The rhino nodded down to the steaks. "I can get you some of these if you want."

The lion's tongue swept over his lips, and he was about to speak, but then the rhino's wife called over to her husband

"It's a yes!"

The lion looked over at his wife who was nodding and smiling, and he frowned.

"What's a yes?"

The rhino grinned. "Apparently the wives have decided we're takin a trip."

"Who?"

"The four of us."

The lion didn't say anything.

"Ten days on the Serengeti — the old country."

The lion looked over at his wife who was smiling wide.

"Maybe we should talk it over first," he said. "I can't just up and leave the company."

"Bullshit," the rhino said. He poked at the steaks with the tongs and moved them around the grill. The smell wafted past the lion's nose.

"No, I'd need to figure things out—really," the lion said. In his head he was calculating the costs—flight, hotels, food—and the more he calculated the more he was hurt by his wife's smile. "I don't know."

The rhino chugged down his beer. "When's the last time you been on vacation?"

"We just got back from the northern zoo." The lion glanced over to his wife.

"Caged!" the rhino said. "Don't you wanna see 'em in their natural habitat up close?"

"Oh I don't know," the lion said.

"Ain't your brother over there?" the rhino said.

"And his sister," the lion's wife said.

"When's the last time you saw them?" the rhino asked.

The lion shrugged.

"Years," his wife said. And she smiled. That smile that hurt the lion in his chest.

"Alright, then," he said.

The rhino slapped him on the shoulder. "Good on ya," he said, then turned back to the barbecue and poked at the steaks.

The lion sipped his beer and turned his back to his wife. "So how much is this gonna cost?"

"It ain't cheap." The rhino shrugged. "But you can't half-ass a trip like that. No point going all that way. What've you gotta worry about, Mr. Moneybags?"

"Oh, I worry just as much as the next guy," the lion said.

The rhino frowned. Then he leaned in.

"You alright?"

"Fine."

"You sure?"

"The industry's not what it used to be."

The rhino played with the steaks, moving them around the grill for no reason other than to keep his back to the wives.

"You got investments?"

"Gone," the lion said. "Cashed in to keep me afloat—mostly went to payroll."

"Savings?"

The lion huffed. "Gone."

The rhino looked over at the wives sipping their drinks in the sun.

"And she don't know."

"No," the lion said.

The steaks sizzled on the grill. The rhino glanced over to the wives again, then back to the lion.

"Suppose I tell you I know a way you could pay for the whole thing—in cash."

The lion perked up, then quickly glanced back to his wife, who was in another conversation, giggling again.

"How?"

The rhino leaned in closer. "You come with me next weekend and this trip will look like chump change."

. . .

Chump change. That's what the rhino had said. The lion is thinking of that now as the truck speeds along the dirt road. He grips the dashboard tighter, pressing his paws firmly against it but careful not to sink his claws into it.

"Slow down—I mean it!"

The rhino laughs and eases up on the gas.

"Why the bug up your arse? Relax," the rhino says. "You got nothin' to worry about."

"What if we get caught?"

"*Relax,*" the rhino says again. "As long as you do exactly what I say then everything will be fine. Do you understand?"

The lion notices how formal the rhino has said this.

"I understand."

"Now, I know you don't hunt much," the rhino continues. "But you've shot a rifle before, right?"

"Not since we were kids," the lion says. "Pop cans and branches and whatever else we could hit. Remember that?"

"This ain't pop cans," the rhino says. "You can ruin a pop can. This target you gotta be exact, otherwise it ain't worth shit. We might as well be shooting dollar bills. You understand?"

The lion nods.

"But don't you worry," the rhino says. "When we're sitting back on the Serengeti sipping a few cold ones I'll let you pay for a round or two."

The truck slows and turns off the dirt road, onto a narrow, overgrown path. The lion rolls up his window to keep from getting whipped by the branches. The truck drives very slow, dipping and bumping and sinking in and out of the path, which in places seems to be no path at all, until they come to a small clearing and stop.

They climb out of the truck. There are only the sounds of the forest, the rustling of leaves high up in the tall trees, the singing of birds and the crickets, dense now in the coming evening.

The rhino flips the front seat forward and grabs the two rifles and lays them across the hood. He takes his pack, which holds a box of cartridges, some loose plastic bags, a canteen of water, a packet of chewing tobacco, a thermos, and some food. Then they head into the bush.

The lion keeps close, his paws out to catch the branches that whip off the rhino.

"Where is it we're going?"

"I know a spot," the rhino says. "It's an old spot but with a bit of luck there might be something there today. If not, we'll go somewhere else."

"How many spots you got?" the lion asks.

"I got a few."

"So where do you find them?" the lion asks as a branch whips back and catches his mane.

"It's all who you know."

"The black market," the lion says.

The rhino shrugs. "It's a market; that's all I know. Don't know what colour it is and don't care." He holds a branch back, then lets it go, and the lion ducks to avoid it.

A fawn and a moose make their way through thick brush, and though the fawn is abnormally little, he keeps up to the moose, who towers over him.

"How you doing, kid? You good?"

"I'm good," the fawn says.

"Am I going too fast?"

"No."

"Alright then," the moose says, and he starts off again. He stops every so often, turning to a porcupine, who has a camera on his shoulder. "If you can get the clearing in the background it'd be good." He places the bows and their quivers on the ground and steps back to frame the shot. "Yeah, right here. Set up right here with the kid to the left, me to the right."

The porcupine signals he is ready and the moose clears his throat and speaks into the camera in a low voice, barely above a whisper.

"Is my mic on?"

The porcupine, wearing headphones now, nods.

The moose peers down at the fawn.

"You ready, kid?"

The fawn straightens up.

The moose clears his throat again and faces the camera, and in his low voice, he begins.

"Today we're in big game country and boy am I excited. I'm joined by my little friend here—" he crouches and pats the fawn on the shoulder then turns back to the camera "—and we're heading down into the clearing behind me, then back up the other side. I know a little spot where we should find a beauty; I've scouted this area for a while now and he's been there most days. A big shout-out to our great sponsor Over Armor for suiting us up; it's a bit chilly and wow we love these fine jackets they've provided us with today." He peers down to the fawn again and grins. "You ready?"

The fawn nods.

"Alright then," the moose says, and with his trademark phrase, he smiles into the camera. "Giddy up!" He pauses for a second, holding still, then relaxes. "How's that?" he asks the porcupine.

"Good light, nice shot," the porcupine says. He checks the camera's battery, then looks up to the sky. "Should be plenty of good light today."

They move along through the forest. The hill is easy at the top but as they descend into the clearing it is steep in places and the footing is loose and the moose slips a little, and he turns to the fawn who seems to be making along just fine. He's a capable little bugger, the moose thinks. He stops before the clearing, instructs the porcupine to set up once again, this time with a specific patch of forest behind them. Then, he leans in and speaks quietly into the camera.

"If you look just over my shoulder, across the clearing and just beyond the tree line, you'll see those sparkling trees." He stands back up. "Get a good shot of that; the sun really makes them sparkle. Zoom in slow, but make sure you start with the clearing." He gets back into position, his face close to the camera again. "Let's hope our target is gonna be there today."

They hike down the hillside toward the clearing.

"Once we're back in the trees we're gonna go into stealth mode," the moose says. "No talking from that point."

"I'll be quiet," the fawn assures him.

"You move well for a midget," the moose says.

The fawn smiles. "My dad taught me to move through the forest."

"Your dad likes to hunt, eh?"

"He takes me out all the time," the fawn says.

"Does he watch the show?"

"Every week," the fawn says. "He told me to get your autograph."

The moose chuckles. "That can be arranged."

Once they reach the clearing, the fawn sees the sparkling trees clearly; a whole section of the forest lit up.

"What's that?"

"You'll see," the moose says. He turns to the porcupine. "Get some B-roll here. Good spot for it — the clearing, up the other side, and the trees too — good light on those trees right now."

The porcupine has already planted his feet into the soft earth of the clearing floor.

"I'm on it."

...

The fawn's father was an old buck with a big set of antlers; not as big as the moose, naturally, but for a buck he was enormous. Those who knew him knew there was nothing more important to him than his dwarf son. The audition tape, which the fawn and his father had recorded three months prior, was something they'd worked hard on.

"Go on now," his father's voice had said from behind the camera.

The fawn had his big bow slung over his shoulder, his quiver and arrows over his other shoulder as he made his way through the narrow trail, and from the angle of the camera, you could not see how little he actually was.

The fawn stopped, and in a split second he'd reached around, pulled his bow, slung an arrow and turned and fired and hit, to his far right, a small bag of grain hanging from a tree forty yards out, which the camera revealed a second later, the arrow in the bag and the bag swaying in the tree.

"Atta boy," the buck's voice said, and when the camera came back he was well behind the fawn, who had moved on, and now you could see he was the size of a fawn half his age. "Why do you want to be on *The Bow Show*?"

"Well," the fawn said, trying to remember his lines. "I was recently named Regional Under-12 Champion."

"Go on," the buck said.

"And a Junior Provincial Champion," the fawn said into the camera. His eyes shifted toward his father, then back to the camera. "And I know I can hit just about anything at any distance. It just comes naturally to me."

"Atta boy," the buck said again.

. . .

The moose was the most famous bow hunter who ever lived; the author of half a dozen bestsellers on the art of bow hunting, TV celebrity, and host of the longest-running and most successful show on Hunting Television, *The Bow Show*.

The show's producer, a quick-witted, fast-talking fox, sat behind his desk, facing the intern, who was a pretty and perky rabbit.

"We've whittled it down to three candidates, sir," the rabbit said. She placed a folder on the fox's desk.

The fox scooted forward in his chair and opened the folder.

"The first," the rabbit said. "Is a cougar. Champion bow hunter. Comes from a poor family."

The fox nodded.

"Poor is good."

"Yes, sir," the rabbit said. "The second is a young tiger, female, immigrant parents."

"That works too," the fox said. "We could run with the whole immigrant thing; the hardships, fitting in—and female? Well, that's gravy. How many female bow hunters are out there? Not many. Is she from a poor family?"

"It doesn't appear so, sir."

"Shit."

"The third," the rabbit said. "Is a fawn. Raised by a single father—"

"Meh," the fox said. "It's been done a thousand times."

"—who is a dwarf."

The fox perked up.

"Who? The father?"

"No, sir, the fawn."

"A midget?"

"Yes, sir."

The fox flopped back in his chair. "Have we ever had one of them on the show?"

"A fawn, sir?"

"No, a midget."

"I don't think so, sir. But the proper terminology is *dwarf* or *little one*."

"Right, right," the fox said, nodding to himself. "Can he walk?"

"Of course, sir. He's just little."

"Is it noticeable?"

"Very much so, sir," the rabbit said. "And yes. He has an awkward way of moving. Kind of a hop and a jump."

"Good," the fox said. "Can't have him carried."

"No, sir," the rabbit said.

The fox lit a cigarette. "Send me those three auditions tapes. But I gotta say, the midget kid sounds like gold. You show the moose yet?"

"No, sir."

"Show him."

"All three?"

"No, just the midget."

"*Dwarf*, sir."

"Right."

The moose appeared in the doorway. He had a huge set of antlers, and he walked with a swagger. He winked at the rabbit, as he always did.

"Whatta ya got for me?"

"We got a gimp," the fox said.

"A gimp?"

The fox, with the cigarette in his mouth, grinned wide. "A midget fawn."

"A midget?"

"Just a little bugger," the fox said.

"Can he shoot?"

The rabbit waited for the moose and the fox to look at her.

"Yes, sir." She did not correct their terminology.

The moose furrowed his brow in thought. "He in a wheelchair? That could be tricky."

"Of course not, sir," the rabbit said. "He is the same as you and me. He is more than capable. He's just little."

The fox was still grinning."Gimps are good. Remember the numbers when we had that one-winged eagle a couple years back?"

"I remember," the moose said. "Nearly killed one of our camera guys. Grazed him on a false release."

"But easily edited and none the wiser," the fox said. "Numbers through the roof."

"Alright then," the moose said.

"You wanna see the tape?" the fox said.

"Have you seen it?"

"No."

The moose turned to the rabbit.

"You're sure he can shoot?"

"Yes, sir. He's an excellent shooter."

"Then I don't need to see it."

The fox smacked his paws together. "The gimp it is!"

...

The fawn and the moose trek across the clearing and hike into the shade of the trees. The fawn shivers and zips up his jacket—his spiffy new *Bow Show* jacket he'd been given back at the studio. It is much too big for him but he is proud of it. He walks right past the second camera operator, a panther who'd managed to cross the clearing unseen and had set up so that he'd shot them emerging from the light and into the shade. The panther knows it is a good shot and he is pleased as he quietly makes his way forward once again.

They hike for a few minutes and then stop. The porcupine sets up his shot, kneeling close to the moose who is on his knees, crouched behind a big tree. The moose looks into the camera and speaks in a whisper.

"About a hundred yards in, you'll see the sparkle in the trees and the trail leading up to them."

The porcupine pans his camera over to the trees. The moose pauses.

"We're gonna keep off the trail and stay below it, and once we come up, if we're lucky, he'll be right where he was yesterday, under them same trees, and—" he nudges the fawn "—our little sharp-shooter here should have a nice, clean shot."

When they get to the desired spot, they see the man standing by one of the trees. They crouch and watch as he picks up a fallen can and places it on a low branch. The porcupine sets up the camera.

The moose leans low to the fawn.

"You ready?" he whispers.

The fawn nods.

The moose makes sure the porcupine has the shot ready, then he nudges the fawn, who pulls his bow, aims carefully, and releases the arrow.

"Oh, you got him!" the moose cries. "Oh you got him good, but he's moving."

The man has scurried up the trail, toward the hillside. The moose leads the fawn to where he'd hit him.

"Plenty of blood," the moose says. "It won't be too hard tracking him." He nods to the porcupine.

"Get some B-roll of the blood. Get in there close before it seeps into the ground."

— 3 —

A young black bear lets out a long, winded sigh. His stepfather, a polar bear, unzips the backpack and hands him a honey sandwich. The cub peels away the neatly folded plastic wrap, like it's a gift. He peels each side of the sandwich; first the top, then the sides, before laying it across his belly. Then, grabbing the first piece and feeling its weight, the bread now dense with honey, and biting the piece in half and tasting the sweetness and the grainy density of the bread, he thinks, as a doughy clump of bread and honey sticks to the roof of his mouth, that if he had to pick a favourite food, this was it.

They are settled in, waiting. Their rifles are perched between them.

The cub sighs again.

"How long do we have to wait?"

"As long as it takes," the polar bear says. He speaks softly. "Be patient. You not having fun?"

The cub shrugs. "Are you sure there's one over there?"

"Yes," the polar bear says.

"Why don't we just go in and get him?"

"Patience," the polar bear says.

"Can't I just take a shot?" the cub asks.

"You'll scare him," the polar bear says.

"Then why not scare him out?"

"No. We wait. That way he will come out slowly and you'll get your shot. Eat your sandwich. Get comfortable. We could be here a while." They sit a moment without speaking. "You know, when I was a cub I got picked on at school too."

The cub perks up. "You did?"

"I did," the polar bear says. "I wasn't a strong athlete; I mean, I was big and strong, but I was clumsy as hell. One time in swimming class I nearly drowned. Back then they made you swim under big blocks of ice."

"You mean icebergs?"

"No, not that big. But big enough that if you lost your way you could be in trouble."

The cub eats his honey sandwich. "What happened?"

"I lost my way," the polar bear says. "The teacher, an old fart of a beaver, had to jump and guide me out. Polar bears are supposed to be good swimmers, but not me." He nods, half to himself. "I never heard the end of it."

"They call you names?" the cub asks.

"Yup."

"Like what?"

The polar bear grins. "*The White-tanic.*"

"*White-tanic?*"

"Yup. That was a good one actually."

"What did you do?"

"Well," the polar bear says. "I socked an elk who made the mistake of calling me that to my face."

"Really?"

The polar bear nods, thinking of it.

"Oh man, I hit him so hard he fell back into one of his buddies and they got their antlers all tangled up."

They both share a quiet chuckle.

...

"Listen," the polar bear had said, leaning against the bedroom door. "You can't do that to other kids at school. You just can't."

The cub sat curled up on the bedroom floor at the foot of the bed, his back turned. He was scowling.

"You don't get it," he said.

"Don't get what?" the polar bear said. "Don't get that you beat up a badger so bad he had to go to the hospital? Or that I got called from work because the police were at your school? Or because you've been suspended three days—THREE days." He grunted. "Which one is it? Tell me that."

"You don't know what they say."

"I don't care what they say," the polar bear said. "I care about how you act."

"That's just it," the cub said. "You don't care."

The polar bear sighed.

"Tell me what they said again."

"They call me *white chocolate*."

The polar bear frowned.

"White chocolate, right. What's that supposed to mean?"

The cub turned.

"You really don't get it? Ever since you married mom that's what everyone calls me."

His mother, a beautiful black bear, appeared in the doorway and rested her head against the polar bear's shoulder.

"Honey," she said to her cub. "Baby. You can't go around fighting everyone that says something you don't like."

"The hyenas laugh at me every day."

"Hyenas are assholes," the polar bear said. "The lot of them."

"What about the badgers?" the cub said.

"Assholes too," the polar bear said.

"Now, now," the black bear said, her voice calm. She stepped into the bedroom. The cub's back was still turned.

"It's not fair," he said. "I didn't ask for this. You were the ones who got married — not me"

"Honey," the black bear said. She looked back and ushered for the polar bear to leave them alone. When he was gone, she knelt at the foot of the bed. "We've talked about this."

The cub turned sharply. "No, YOU talked. I never said anything."

"OK," she said. "Talk."

"He's not like us," the cub said. "You know he's not."

"We are all different in our own ways."

"You know what I mean," the cub said. "Moving here, into this house, changing schools. Polar bears and black bears aren't supposed to get married. Look at hyenas; they stick together."

"Nobody but a hyena would marry a hyena," the black bear said, grinning.

The cub did not grin back.

"You know what I mean," he said again.

Later that evening, with the cub asleep in his room, the black bear and the polar bear lay in bed with the light on.

"I'm worried about him," the black bear said. She had her head on the pillow and was staring up at the ceiling.

"He'll be fine," the polar bear said.

The black bear shook her head.

"No," she said. "I mean it. First it was his grades, and now he's beating up his classmates. He's acting like...."

"Like a hyena," the polar bear said, and chuckled.

The black bear turned onto her side, so that she faced him.

"You two need to do something together. A father-son thing."

"He'll never see me as his father," the polar bear said. "He's too old for that now."

"Well, you're the only one he's got," she said. "He's old enough to know his real father wants nothing to do with him. Lord knows the damage that's caused. What do we do? Do we see a psychiatrist?"

The polar bear huffed. "Some wise-ass owl charging two-hundred bucks an hour? What good is that gonna do?"

"I don't know," she said. "I've run out of ideas."

"Maybe I can figure something out for us to do," the polar bear said.

The next day, the polar bear stood at the bedroom door again. The cub was on his bed, playing a video game.

"Come to the garage for a second," the polar bear said. He nodded to the game console. "Put that away."

The cub quietly sighed, but it was enough for the polar bear to notice. He climbed off his bed and followed the polar bear into the garage.

There was a big steel cabinet along the wall. The cub had never seen inside it before, and he watched as the polar bear slid the key into the padlock, turned it with a click, and opened it up. The polar bear was huge but the cabinet towered over him, all the way up to the ceiling, and ever since the cub and his mother moved into this house, the cabinet in the garage had always been a mysterious and untouchable thing. And so, when the latch clicked open, he stood with bated breath. He knew there were guns inside—his step-father hunted, but he had never shown the cub any of his guns; and then the cabinet door opened and there were five guns in all. Four were hunting rifles, and there was an assault rifle. The polar bear stepped back and allowed the cub a moment to just look, before he pulled out a black, sniper rifle.

"This here," he said, a hint of pride in his voice. "Is a Remington 700."

The cub stood, mouth slightly agape.

The polar bear offered it to the cub. "Be careful with it. It's not a toy."

The cub did not say a word as he held the rifle, not knowing whether to hold it up and look through the scope, or just hold it as it was, upright. The polar bear removed the soft shell covering off the scope, then, gently, he raised the gun so that the stock rested against the cub's shoulder.

"Keep it snug," he said. "Otherwise it'll kick back and boy, that'll hurt."

The cub held it just as he was instructed.

"Now tilt your head a little," the polar bear said.

The cub peered through the scope, squinting, the rifle aimed out the garage door, past the driveway, to the house across the street.

"It's blurry."

"Slide your head back a bit," the polar bear whispered, an intimacy now between them.

The cub slid his head back a little, and, still squinting, the woodwork of the house came into view, clearly, as if by magic, as though he were standing right in front of it. He lifted his head and looked across the street.

The polar bear chuckled.

"Pretty neat, eh?"

"It's so clear," the cub said.

The polar bear nodded.

"That's a Keeley Diamondback. Best scope on the market. That thing can spot a zit on a porcupine's arse from two hundred yards."

The cub looked through the scope again, this time going beyond the house and into the backyard, where he settled on the tree line. The polar bear gently adjusted the scope.

"Pick something. Tell me when it comes into focus."

A second or two passed.

"There—" the cub said.

"What do you see?"

The cub held the gun perfectly still.

"A leaf."

"A leaf?"

"A leaf," the cub muttered. "On the big maple tree." He pretended to fire, making the sound of a gunshot. He handed the rifle back to the polar bear, who put the cap back on the scope and placed the rifle in its slot in the cabinet. He then grabbed what looked like the oldest rifle of the lot; the stock was worn and unpolished and had a small chip. He turned to the cub.

"This here is my favorite rifle. You don't get much more reliable than this .308." He took a moment, turning it over in his hands. "My dad gave this to me. Got my first kill with it the same day I got it. I was about your age. Up north."

He handed the rifle to the cub. It felt like a toy gun compared the previous rifle. The polar bear turned back to the cabinet, pulled a small tin box and opened it. He showed the cub what was inside.

The cub frowned at the discolored clump of dried flesh.

"What is it?"

"Earlobe," the polar bear said. "For good luck. From a young Eskimo. Came right up into the back-yard looking for food. They're dangerous when they're hungry. My dad let me take the shot. First shot I ever fired from that rifle. It was right outta the box. Boy, it was something." He paused, thinking of it, lost for a few seconds. "Suppose we went hunting, just the two of us. You think that'd be something you'd want to do? My dad—" he stopped abruptly. "I'm not pretending to be your dad, I'm only saying…My dad used to take me out all the time."

The cub's eyes widened before looking down at the floor, deflated. He handed the .308 back to the polar bear.

"Mom would never let me."

The polar bear grinned.

"What if I told you I've already talked to her?"

The cub perked up.

The polar bear nodded.

"And she's fine with it."

"She is?"

The polar bear shrugged lightheartedly.

"Well, she's given me some instructions," he said, then winked. "You know your mother."

...

They left just before dawn. The polar bear had packed honey sandwiches, apples, and juice. He'd woken the cub out of a dead sleep and the cub had slumped in the car as they drove, and it wasn't long before he was asleep again, his head back, snout raised, and snoring. The polar bear knew the exact spot he would take the cub; the same place he'd first hunted when he'd moved here. It was a changed territory now, the land cleared and structures raised, but it was a populous area and he hoped it would ensure a successful hunt. He remembered back to when he was a cub, living up North, when the young Eskimo had wandered into the yard, and how he'd perched himself against the edge of the house and his father had whispered in his ear as he aimed. Breathe, he'd told him. Breathe, son, and as you exhale, relax your body and only when you know you are relaxed, when your heart has settled, squeeze the trigger. And when he set his sights on the mark, square in the middle of the young Eskimo's chest, and breathed as he was told, his father's voice warm and secretive in his ear, he squeezed the trigger and the rifle gave a crack and the Eskimo slumped forward and fell face down in the snow.

"A fine shot," his father had said, and he knelt over the Eskimo and sliced off the earlobe. "We will dry this in the shed, and you will have it to remember this, your first one, and it will bring you good luck."

The polar bear needed that luck now, he knew, as he drove, feeling the stiffness of the earlobe snug against his chest, tucked into his breast pocket, the cub snoring beside him. *White chocolate*, he thought, and chuckled.

It was still dark outside when he parked the car. He turned around and reached for the backpack with the lunches, then went into the trunk and grabbed the two rifles— his own and the .308— before opening the passenger door and gently nudging the cub.

"We're here," he said.

The cub rubbed his eyes, yawned and stretched before climbing out of the car.

"Here," the polar bear said, handing him the .308. "You carry your own gun."

The polar bear looked up at the stars; it was a clear night sky and the moon was bright. He took a deep breath.

"Nothing like the fresh early-morning air. Breathe it in—it'll wake you up. Now come on, we've got a bit of a hike in front of us."

They were on the other side of the highway, hidden in the tall grass. There was a thin line of pink on the horizon.

"Over there," the polar bear said, pointing across the highway, to the big glass buildings in the distance. He leaned low and, gripping with his claws, he cleared some dirt and lifted a big metal cover and looked into the darkness below. "Ready?"

The cub nodded. His stomach growled with hunger.

The polar bear lowered himself into the hole and the cub followed. They descended a long way down a metal ladder, into the darkness. With their flashlights they could make out the narrow cement walk next to slow-flowing water and the maze of pipe-works overhead.

"Be careful," the polar bear said. "Some of those pipes might be hot." His voice echoed in the closeness of the pipeworks. The tunnel smelled of metal and oil.

The cub held his flashlight a little higher now, following the rows of pipes, some rattling and shaking.

"We're right over the highway now," the polar bear said.

They continued through the tunnel that twisted and turned, until they climbed a ladder and emerged through the floor of an electrical room and into a parking garage where they hid behind a parked car. Then they sat.

"Now we wait," the polar bear said. "It's early."

They sat for almost an hour.

"There's the stairwell," the polar bear said. "No talking from this point."

The cub nodded.

They rushed across the well-lit underground lot and through a heavy door and into a stairwell. They waited a moment, listening. The stairwell was empty. They climbed. And they climbed. The cub's legs were twitchy by the time they got to the tenth floor. The polar bear put his ear to the door.

"Stay close to me," he whispered, and pulled open the door and was surprised by a maintenance worker smoking a cigarette in the upper stairwell. The polar bear cocked his rifle and fired two shots and the maintenance worker fell forward and tumbled down the stairs. The two shots cracked loud in the stairwell. Then the hallway door burst open and the polar bear turned and fired off a shot but missed another man, the bullet ricocheting off the door before it slammed shut. And soon there were screams from the other side of the door. The polar bear grabbed the cub and they rushed up a flight of stairs and waited. They could still hear screaming from the lower floor.

"Goddammit!" the polar bear said.

They waited until it was quiet again. The cub stayed close to the polar bear. Wide-eyed. Not speaking.

...

The cub takes another bite of his honey sandwich. He is grinning.

"*White-tanic*, eh? What happened to the elk after you hit him?"

"I got in shit," the polar bear says. "Not so much from my father but from the school. Suspension for a day or two—just like you. My father was more upset at the whole situation—me being a weak swimmer, the name calling, the whole thing. He was a proud bear, and he never mentioned the elk."

"Did he stop?"

"Who?"

"The elk."

"Oh yeah. They all stopped after that."

"So you don't think it's wrong what I did to the badger?"

"Between you and me, the little bastard got what he deserved." He turns to the cub, who is finishing his honey sandwich. "You got him good?"

The cub grins again.

"Knocked out two of his teeth."

"Ha!" the polar bear laughs, then covers his mouth, realizing he'd laughed loud. "Probably did him a favour," he says, his voice low. "Badgers and their damned teeth. And when you get back to school if the hyenas laugh at you, hit one of them too."

"Seriously?"

"Seriously."

"Mom will kill me."

The polar bear shrugs. "She'll kill me first. And while she's killing me you'll have a chance to escape."

And they chuckle quietly.

The polar bear reaches into the backpack for an apple.

"So what do you think of all this?"

The cub peers out across the open space. "It's not bad. I mean this, hanging out."

The polar bear nods.

There is a brief silence between them.

"I'm sorry," the cub says. "I like it at your house. Mom's happy."

The polar bear grunts, eats the apple, and adjusts himself into position.

"Let's get focused. He'll be coming out soon."

PART 3

—1—

"You're doing great, Kate."

Kate slips her head behind the hanging dress and feels the soft, feather-light material on her face and nestles herself as tight as she can into the corner of the closet.

"Do you hear anything?" the operator asks.

"Nothing right now."

"Police are on the way," the operator says. "Just stay where you are."

Kate is crying, sobbing, her body shaking, quietly, muffling her sobs into her shirt sleeve.

"My babies," she says, thinking of them, of what they must be doing right now, huddled together in the dirt and darkness of the den under the fallen tree.

"Where are your children?" the operator asks. It is almost annoying to Kate how calm the operator is, and she wishes she were on the other end of the line, in that room, or that cubicle. She wipes her eyes and nose onto her damp shirt sleeve.

"They're safe for now." She gets another whiff of bleach in the closet and her mind wanders once again back to the afternoon, just a few hours ago, but how far away it seems now; how impossibly far away it seems and feels, and thinking of it now, she searches for it again, for the safety in the distance of it.

"Breakfast for dinner?" she said after the kitchen was clean enough to eat in; the cupboards all scrubbed down, the linoleum floor mopped, the fridge cleaned—it had been the hardest thing to clean, smelling strongly of the festering emptiness of it; of the plastic shelves and old bits of dried-out spills; she'd had to use bleach to rid it, and she was pleased with the clean, bleachy smell when she was finished. She'd emptied the cooler and had put bacon, eggs, margarine, and some juice boxes in the fridge.

"I want pancakes," Timothy said.

"Sure," Kate said. "And bacon and eggs."

Timothy licked his lips.

"I like breakfast for dinner," he said. He paused. "But if we're having it for dinner then it's no longer breakfast, which means it's not breakfast for dinner."

Kate smiled."Then what is it?"

Timothy shrugged."It's just dinner."

"I want pancakes too!" Ruby said.

Kate opened the big Dollar Store bag she'd brought in from the car: one small frypan, three plates, a handful of forks, knives, and spoons, three mugs, and a spatula.

She opened the newly cleaned, bleach-smelling fridge and grabbed the eggs, bacon, and margarine. Next she stirred the pancake mix, adding tap water to the bowl, which she'd run for twenty minutes before it was clear; it had first come out brown.

There'd been some canned food in the cupboards: beans, apricots, and a can of maple syrup, and she threw them out, but she'd bought syrup at the Dollar Store too, and a few cans of soup.

Timothy and Ruby devoured their pancakes.

"More!" they said, laughing, drumming the butts of their forks on the table.

"Hold on," Kate said, grinning. "I've got to get this bacon cooked first. We really need to buy another frypan."

The salty, greasy smell of the frying bacon quickly engulfed the bleachy smell but gave the kitchen life; it was a working kitchen again. The grease spattered on the stove top.

"I like it here," Timothy said.

Ruby drank her milk, the mug covering her tiny face, which sat level with the table's edge.

"Me too!"

Kate flipped the bacon with a fork, careful not to get any grease on her clothes.

...

"I'm scared," Kate whispers into the phone.

"Ok," the operator says. "Just stay where you are. And stay quiet."

"Then stop talking to me!" Kate hisses. Then: "I'm sorry. I'm sorry."

"It's OK," the operator says. "The police are on the way."

"Don't leave me."

"I'm right here."

"Please don't leave me," Kate says again.

"You're going to be fine," the operator says.

Again, Kate hears the dry tone of the voice on the other end of the phone; the line delivered; shift work; lines rehearsed and delivered daily so many times that any empathy had all but drained away. Kate pulls her knees closer to her chest.

...

A branch flings back and catches the lion in the eye and he stops. He and the rhino are in thick brush and the rhino doesn't realize the lion has stopped, and he turns.

"You there?"

"Yeah," the lion says. "Branch got me. Gimme a sec."

The mosquitoes and blackflies are thick and the rhino swats them away as he waits.

"You alright?"

The lion rubs his eye with the back of his paw, and then he blinks and his eye tears up and he blinks a couple more times before his vision clears.

"Yeah, yeah," he says, pushing the branches aside, until he rejoins the rhino, who is smiling at him.

"You won't be complaining once we're sippin' beers on the Serengeti."

"I shoulda just put it on the credit card," the lion says.

"Oh, but you can't afford it," the rhino says.

The lion huffs and shakes his head, and they move on through the thick brush again, until, as though pulling back a curtain, they step into a flat pine-needled forest floor. Through the trees, a small clearing comes into view, and beyond it, a hayfield. They step out of the forest and into the clearing, which has about a dozen old, rusted cars.

"Up there," the rhino points.

The field slopes upward, and at the line where the field and sky meet, there is the back of a barn, and the roof of a house, and the green of the cluster of trees surrounding the property.

The rhino sits on a rusted bumper of one of the cars, gets out his thermos, and pours some coffee into the lid.

"We wait till dusk," he says. "Then we'll make our way up the edge of the field, along the hay." He digs into his pack and unwraps a sandwich. "Make yourself comfortable. We got some time."

The lion sits on the ground, digs into his pack, and pulls out his thermos.

"You gonna be able to do this right?" the rhino asks. "Don't you be all shaking and shit when it comes time to pull the trigger. You gotta be calm and do it right."

"I know, I know," the lion says. He uncaps his thermos and pours some coffee into the lid and sips.

"Let's go through it one more time," the rhino says. "Where do you shoot?"

The lion taps his chest.

"Right here," he says. "Right in the middle."

"And nowhere else," the rhino says. "Whatever you do, NEVER a headshot. You'll risk shattering the teeth. You might as well piss your profit away. And any blood in the hair and it'll be worthless. It'll stain it. And I don't wanna spend all goddam weekend going through every strand of hair trying to clean it out." He sips his coffee and bites into the sandwich. "We're in and out quick. We take the head, fingernails and toenails — that's it. We could take the hide but it's not worth the effort."

"I got it," the lion says.

"You sure? You don't sound sure."

"Yeah, I'm sure."

"Think of your wife," the rhino says. "Think of the Serengeti."

The lion is thinking of the trip, imagining it; the vastness of the Serengeti, of the relatives he'll see. His brother had told them he'd meet them at the airport, and he is excited about seeing him, but it doesn't make him feel any better about what they are doing.

"This isn't easy for me," he says. "This kind of thing."

"If it was easy everyone would be doing it," the rhino says. He finishes his sandwich and tosses the wrapper onto the ground. "But I get it. I didn't like it much the first time I did it either."

"But you like it now?" the lion asks.

The rhino shrugs. "Don't like it, but it's easier now. That's all. Don't think. Just do it. And when it's done, put it behind you. Get your money and don't look back."

The sun is setting behind the trees. They wait a good while without speaking. The crickets are loud, and they fill the early evening.

"So, this is a good spot, eh?" the lion finally says.

"As good as I've got," the rhino says.

"You ever get anything here before?"

"Not me, no," the rhino says. "Why? You worried?"

"No."

"Don't worry," the rhino says. "You'll make a killing today, trust me."

"Good," the lion says, though the word feels heavy in his mouth now that it is getting closer. He reaches into his pack for a slice of meat his wife had packed for him. He is not hungry, but he eats it anyway.

Kate feels the wetness of her sleeve and she realizes how much she's cried, and so she forces herself to stop. She cannot hear any voices in the hall. Just the quiet of the house and the closeness of the closet.

"Are you there?" the operator asks.

"Yes," she whispers, so quietly her lips don't move; the words in her breath.

"You're doing great," the operator says.

"Oh shut up, please," Kate says. She starts crying again, not caring that it makes noise.

"Police are on the way."

"Where are they coming from—the fucking moon?"

"They were dispatched from Sussex. It won't be long."

Kate thinks of her children. She knows they got out, having seen them rushing through the hayfield in the darkness, toward the forest. She wonders what they are doing now. Under the fallen tree. Timothy holding tight to Ruby.

"I'm getting off the phone," she whispers.

"Stay on the line, please, Kate."

"No. I'm hanging up."

"Please stay on the line, Kate."

Kate swipes off her phone.

A second later, her phone buzzes. It is very loud, the vibrating in her hand. She answers.

"Don't call me back. You're putting me in more danger."

"Kate, please," the operator says. "It's in your best interest that you stay on the line."

"Why?" Kate says. "So you can hear me getting killed?"

She swipes off the call and goes into her photos, scrolling through them and stopping at one on Lake Ontario from just last week; Ruby clinging to Timothy at the edge of the water, their hair wet and flat, big smiles and eyes squinting in the sun. Just last week. Should you have stayed? No, she thinks, no, no, no. She scrolls through the photos taken in the kitchen just twenty minutes ago.

…

Breakfast for dinner. Ruby with syrup on her chin, her head tilted, level with the tabletop. The smell of bacon grease in the kitchen, flipping the bacon with a fork, careful not to get any grease on her clothes. Her only worry. The grease. It was at that moment she'd spotted the two shadows crossing the courtyard and for a quick second her breath caught in her throat and it felt like a dream where her legs failed to work. But it was only a split second and she moved quickly.

"Get up," she'd said. "Both of you."

Ruby frowned. Her mouth full.

Timothy was frowning too. "Mom, what's wrong?"

Kate placed her hands squarely on Timothy's shoulders.

"You need to go down to the forest, under the tree. Take your sister. Do you understand?"

"But Mom—"

Kate yanked Timothy's chair out from the table. "Go!" she said. "Now!" She grabbed Ruby, who started to cry.

"Mom, you're scaring me," Timothy said.

Kate led them through the back of the house, then opening the screen door and looking quickly around, she shoved them outside and taking Timothy by the shoulders again, she spoke in a low, tense voice.

"Go through the field and don't look back. I will be there soon." She kissed them both hard on the forehead and pushed them away. "Now go!"

She closed the screen door and climbed the stairs and into her bedroom and called 9-1-1.

. . .

Her phone buzzes again.

She smothers it with both hands and buries her hands under her legs. Muzzled, it keeps buzzing. Then it stops. Then it starts again. She hears, through the closet, the bedroom door handle clicking, the door pushed on.

. . .

The rhino looks up at the sky; the sun has settled below the trees and the moon is out. He tucks his thermos into his pack and stands up.

"Alright," he says. "It's time."

The lion uncaps his water bottle and takes a long drink. He stops for a breath and takes another drink.

"You sure you're alright?" the rhino asks.

"I'm good."

The hayfield looks blue in the moonlight as they make their way up the edge of the field. They no longer see the house, hidden behind the bulk of the barn. But there is the white of the yard lights and the silhouettes of the tops of the big trees.

They trek the length of the field and crawl alongside the fence-line and nestle up against the back of the barn. Then they scamper across the open courtyard and kneel under the windows of the front porch. They wait and listen. The house is silent. They step inside the porch. They did not notice, behind them, Timothy and Ruby crossing the courtyard and disappearing behind the barn.

They step into the kitchen. The smell of bacon makes the lion's mouth water. He licks the syrup from one of the plastic plates. They move through the kitchen and into the back room, to the foot of the staircase. The rhino points up the staircase then clicks off the rifle's safety and steps on the first stair. It creaks loud. Every step creaks as they make their way upstairs, then onto the landing, and then down the hall, to the bedroom door. The rhino nods to the door handle. The lion tries it. It is locked. He pushes on the door. His heart is racing, the rifle shaking in his paws.

"What do you think?" the lion asks.

The rhino perches his rifle against the wall. "Move outta the way."

The lion steps aside. The rhino lowers his head and smashes through the bedroom door. It is an explosion in the quiet of the house. The door sways, clinging to a hinge before dropping in a flat, muted thud on the carpet. The lion hands the rhino his rifle and they step into the bedroom. The rhino points his rifle across the room, toward the closet door. The lion, standing behind him, steps to his side and points his rifle. The rhino nods to the safety switch.

The lion clicks it off, then they step toward the closet door, rifles pointed.

—2—

Mel Tinsel can see, down over the hillside, the patch of trees sparkling with the tin cans. From up here, it looks like the trees are made of glass. Blood has run down his leg and into his shoe, and his sock is mushy between his toes. He breathes deeply but feels he's not getting enough air, no matter how deeply he inhales. Through the trees he catches glimpses of the two hunters making their way up the hillside. He gets to his feet. The piece of arrow sticks out from his side. The left side of his body burns, the pain striking in flashes every time he moves.

He can also see Meenan's Cove Road far below. He has two choices: Go straight down the steep hillside and through the thick forest, or move along the top of the hill and down its eastern side, toward Quispamsis Road. It is a busier road and he knows a car would surely come. To his right, the ferry crosses the river, loaded with cars, and there is the small beach and the blurred specks of people laying in the sun and playing in the water. How casual life is outside your own, he thinks, as his side shrieks. He takes another deep breath, and then he hears the voice in the phone.

"Sir — Mel —" the operator says. "Are you there?"

"I'm here," Mel says. The pain from lifting the phone to his ear causes him to buckle. "I'm changing course. I'm going for Quispamsis Road."

"That's good," the operator says. "You can do it. I know you can."

Mel grins a little.

"Son, I'm not going to make it. But I'll try anyway. They're gaining on me. I can see it. But for your sake, I'll try."

"Good then, that's good," the operator says.

Mel cringes as the pain strikes.

"Did you get hold of my boys?"

"They have been called, yes."

"Tell them their old man didn't go down without a fight."

"You can tell them yourself."

Mel grins again. "You're a good kid."

"Thank you, sir — Mel."

"OK then," Mel says, grunting. "Here we go. I'm gonna put the phone in my pocket but I'll keep it on."

He moves as quickly as he can through the trees. In some places there are only a few feet between both sides of the hill, and he moves carefully. But in the places where he can move quickly he does, and sometimes his arm catches the arrow in his side and he stumbles to the ground in pain. He gets up and takes quick deep breaths, easing the pain, then slowly, then quickly again. His lungs burn, and he knows he can go no further. He dips his hand into his pocket for his phone.

"That's it," he says. He can barely speak he is breathing so hard. "I'm done."

"Sir — Mel," the operator says.

"Son, I've lived a good life." He takes a few seconds to catch his breath before speaking again. "No need feeling sorry for me." He crawls to a tree and rests against it. He looks down at the long stretch of the river, at the tiny white of sailboats, and the green of the hills, and the hills farther away, hazy and grey. There is a fast-flowing breeze and it cools in the wetness of his clothes. He wriggles his toes in his mushy sock. Far down the hillside, the cans sparkle in the trees.

"I'm going to see my wife," he says into the phone.

"Sir," the operator says. "Mel—"

Mel tosses the phone and it settles a few feet away, in a mess of pinecones. He keeps his stare on the trees below. It is difficult to focus, trying to flush out the pain, striking him when he breathes, and so he purses his lips and tries to slow his breathing. *Find it,* he tells himself, looking down at his trees below. *Find it and go there.*

He and his wife are uptown, on the Boardwalk. There is a cruise ship in the port. It towers over the buildings along Water Street.

That's the QE2, he says.

They are sitting at a table outside Grannan's. He sips on a cold beer. She has a gin and tonic. Her hair rests on her shoulders and the cool harbour breeze blows the ends, tickling her skin.

When did cruise ships start coming here?

After you died, Mel says.

I bet it brings business, she says.

It does. Especially to the Market. You can't move in there when a ship comes in. Rich folk from New York with their American dollars looking for t-shirts and trinkets.

And a cup of chowder from Lord's.

Ah, yes, Mel says. You do love that chowder.

It's so fresh. And the lobster and cream make my mouth water.

It upsets my stomach, Mel says.

She smiles and sips her gin. Her hair blows a little in the breeze. You say that, but I never saw you try it. Not once.

Mel coughs, and his body burns. There is blood at the corner of his mouth. He wipes it on his pants and focuses on the trees again. In the pinecones, his cell phone rings.

Give me a spoonful then, he says.

She dips the plastic spoon into the Styrofoam cup and reaches across the table with a steaming spoonful and holds it in front of his face.

Be careful, there may be bones in it.

We did good, didn't we? The boys. Our family. Our life.

Yes, we did, she says.

We were happy?

Very happy.

But it went so quickly, he says. Our babies to boys to men to fathers. It went so quickly, one day after another, a year after another, gone in a flash.

It is because it was a good life, she says. Happiness is a fleeting thing. Rarely do you appreciate it before it is gone; you are too busy enjoying it to notice.

He closes his eyes and nods slowly.

It was so good. All of it. And so it ends. But what more is there than that?

There is nothing more than that.

Then I'm ready, he says.

The spoonful of chowder is suspended in front of his face.

Try it, she says.

He grins.

I'm ready, he says again.

I'm right here, she says. Right here. Now eat.

He looks over to the Harbour Bridge and the houses on the West Side and the open water of the bay.

I love you, darling, he says. I love that our boys had you as their mother, and that—" Mel coughs up more blood. A cloud passes and hides the sun and far down the hillside the trees no longer sparkle. His side shrieks and he digs his heels into the ground, his fingernails into the earth, and he closes his eyes again.

I'm cold, he says.

Eat, she says, holding the spoonful of chowder. It'll warm you up.

. . .

The porcupine is crouched, the camera perched upon his shoulder, as the moose shows him a bloodied leaf.

"He's bleedin' pretty good," the moose says. "He won't get too far."

He gets out his binoculars and scans the hillside. It is a nicely framed shot, the moose looking through his binoculars, the little fawn standing beside him, barely half the height of the moose's legs.

"There he is," the moose says. He lowers his voice. "You ain't going nowhere." He turns to the fawn and hands him the binoculars and points. "Up the hill—that big ol' birch poking out where the hill falls off."

The porcupine steps around them and focuses the camera on the fawn.

"Find the birch then work your way to the left," the moose says.

The fawn stands very still, the binoculars locked to his eyes, scanning the hillside.

"I see it," he says.

"Now go to the left, just a bit," the moose says. "You see him? Right in that open patch of rock there, and just below it, at the base of that big spruce."

The fawn takes a moment. The porcupine zooms in close, holding the shot.

"I see him—"

"He's down," the moose says. He pauses then turns to the porcupine. "You get all that?"

The porcupine nods.

The moose crouches to the fawn.

"All we gotta do now is get up the hillside a bit so you can get a clean shot and finish him off. Sound good?"

The fawn nods enthusiastically.

"Alright then," the moose says. He looks at the porcupine again. "We'll come back here when we're done and get some more B-roll. Right now we gotta get up the hill."

The porcupine's tiny head pops out from behind the camera.

"We should get the shots right now, with the sun where it is. If we wait too long it won't be the same."

"Do what you gotta do," the moose says. "But we gotta get up there and get our shot before he gets a second wind and he's gone down the other side."

"I need a few minutes."

The moose looks around. "Where the hell is the panther?"

"I'm over here," the panther says from the bushes.

The moose turns to the porcupine. "Let's go. We need simultaneous shots of the kid and the kill shot. We'll come back here tomorrow if you need more."

The porcupine huffs.

"It's easy to play around with sequence," the moose says.

"And easy to screw it up," the porcupine says. "The viewer needs to be able to follow it."

The moose shrugs. "Fuck the viewer." He looks down to the fawn. "Sorry, kid." He turns back to the porcupine. "We keep the narrative going; keep it interesting and the sequence takes care of itself."

"No," the porcupine says. "The sequence has to be closely watched. One screw up in continuity and the whole thing falls apart."

The moose shrugs again, this time more forcefully.

"It has to tie together," the porcupine says. "Right now it's fragmented."

"That's why we have editors," the moose says. "It don't always gotta tie together. There are no rules. Give them something interesting, something that keeps them watching and be damned with the rules. A story is a story. From start to finish. If it's good it's good and that's all that matters. You think I give a shit what people think? This is our seventh year. I know what I'm doing."

"I don't like it," the porcupine says.

"Well, it's a good thing it's my show then, eh?"

The fawn is still peering through the binoculars.

"He still there?" the moose asks.

The fawn nods.

"Yeah, we got him, kid," the moose says. "Just gotta get within range." He turns to the porcupine and waits for him to mount his camera on his shoulder before speaking again, turning on his charm. "Well we've got ourselves a nice situation here. Our target is down but not out. Our first shot got him in the side and he's been moving, but we've tracked him. We're gonna make our way up the hill a bit, toward that clearing over to the right—" He points toward the hillside. "Then our wee sharpshooter here is gonna be primed for the kill shot." He crouches again to the fawn. "You ready?"

The fawn, eyes wide, nods quickly and the moose looks into the camera again, nostrils flaring as he grins.

"Giddy up!"

...

Mel is shivering, his body stiffening against the base of the big tree. He is no longer in pain. A squirrel skitters down the trunk and leaps over him to the ground, near his outstretched legs, then perks up in a quick jerk, sees Mel and scatters. The sun comes through the clouds and Mel catches another glimpse of the sparkling trees below.

"I'm cold," he says aloud.

What are you thinking of? she asks.

The ice storm.

The year before I died.

Yes.

That was cold, she says.

The candles were so lovely in the kitchen.

Yes.

Mel smiles uncomfortably. If he moves he will hurt, his side will burn and he'll lose focus, and so he stays as still as he can. He purses his lips and breathes.

"Romantic," he says with a grunt.

It was, she says.

We were young and broke and the power was cut in the middle of winter. Our basement apartment. Sydney Street.

Yes.

What a shithole.

She chuckles. But our last house was lovely.

It is, he says.

The forest is quiet for a moment.

Mel shivers.

I'm coming home, he says. I'm ready.

A few feet away, half buried in pine needles, his phone buzzes. The squirrel has returned and sniffs at the ground around it.

"Get it over with," Mel says aloud. The squirrel skitters away. Mel takes a deep breath and the pain surges through him. "I'm here! Do you see me? I'm right here!" The trees rustle in the breeze. Then he chuckles.

What's so funny? she asks.

He chuckles again.

I have to pee.

A few feet away, an arrow lands and plunks into the soft earth.

...

The fawn does his best not to show his struggle up the hillside. The moose has lagged behind with the porcupine, leaving the fawn with the second camera operator, the panther. The moose waits until the fawn is well ahead of them before he turns to the porcupine.

"Listen, do me a favour, will ya? You got an issue with me don't bring it up in front of the kid. It's my gig. You don't like what I'm doing, fine, there's plenty of work with that new beaver home show—"

The porcupine frowns.

"*This Dam House*?"

The moose laughs.

"Is that what it's called?"

"Yeah."

"Shit."

"I got no problem with keeping quiet," the porcupine says. "But gimme some respect. I been here since the beginning too."

"Yeah, I hear ya," the moose says. "But these kids look up to me, you know? That's all." He looks to the fawn and the panther. "That's good right there." They stop. He turns to the porcupine. "This look good to you?"

The porcupine squints a little. Mel is about sixty yards up, at the top of the hill.

"Is he dead?"

"Not sure," the moose says. "But he ain't moving."

The panther moves into the brush and sets up his camera and finds the man against the tree and zooms in. He takes a steady pan of the hillside. Then another. Then he focuses again on the man, who hasn't moved. The porcupine stays with the moose and sets up the shot, placing them in the foreground, with the man showing clearly. It is rare that he has so much time to set up a kill shot, and he is pleased.

"A little to the left," he says.

The moose and the fawn step to the side.

"Perfect."

The moose leans low and puts his arm around the fawn. He speaks softly.

"You think you can make that shot?"

The fawn pulls an arrow from his quiver. It is nearly the length of his body.

"I think so."

"Good. Take your time. He ain't going nowhere." He turns to the porcupine. "Alight, you ready?"

"We're rolling," the porcupine says.

The moose looks into the camera.

"This is it," he whispers. "Our target is just up the hill there. It should be a nice clean shot." He twists around, low to the fawn who has the bow ready. "This kid is one hell of a hunter. But it's still a tough shot uphill with the wind up here."

The fawn lifts his bow and takes aim.

— 3 —

"Seventeen pounds," Terry says into the phone. He is standing upright now. His shirt sticks to his back, wet with sweat.

"Can you repeat that, Terry?" the operator says.

"Seventeen pounds. That's how much weight I've lost since I left Longo's."

"That's good, Terry."

"Do you know how hard it is to lose seventeen pounds?" His heart flutters. "I'm going to ask out a girl. I'm going to Longo's tonight and I'm gonna ask her out."

"That's good, Terry," the operator says again. "What are you doing right now? Are you under the desk?"

"I'm getting outta here," Terry says.

"Terry, that's not a good idea."

Terry is nodding. "Oh, it is. There's nobody here. The elevators aren't far away."

"Get under the desk, Terry. Please."

The room is empty, just the cubicles and the buzzing of the overhead lights. It reminds Terry of the mornings he arrives before anyone else. It is only for a few minutes before the doors open and someone else comes in. But for the short time he is alone in the room he enjoys the silence, waiting for the day to get started. But now it is a different silence.

"There's nobody here," he says into the phone.

"Terry, get back under the desk."

"It's OK. There's nobody here."

"Terry, please listen to me. You need to get back under the desk and stay there until SWAT clears the building. They know where you are. They will be there soon."

Then something comes over Terry. A flash of hot whiteness. It starts in his toes and shoots up his legs and into his chest and down his arms and into his fingers. He feels ten feet tall.

"I've been hiding too long," he says.

"Terry, just a few minutes more."

"No, I mean hiding forever."

"I don't follow you, Terry."

Terry stands a bit taller and takes a deep breath, inflating his chest. He actually smiles.

"I've always done what people tell me to do. I've never made a single decision in all my life. Ever. Do you know that I had this day planned? That every day I've starved myself and I've woken up and stood on the scale and told myself a few more pounds. A few more then I'm gonna do it. I'm gonna ask her out. I woke up today and I decided that today is the day and nothing is gonna stop me. I'm walking out of here. This ends now."

"Terry, listen to me. Please get back under the desk."

Terry swipes off his phone and puts it in his pocket.

He steps out from behind the partition of the manager's office and into the openness of the rows of cubicles. He walks, for the first time in his life, in his own shoes; he does not feel fat. He feels big. He does not feel shy. He feels strong. Invincible. Alive.

...

The cub licks his lips. "Any more honey sandwiches?"

The polar bear digs into his pack and pulls out another sandwich and hands it to the cub.

"So we just sit here?" the cub asks.

"Yup."

"That's it?"

"Hunting isn't just about shooting," the polar bear says. "It's about patience. The real hunter enjoys all of the experience. You not having fun?"

"It's fine."

Neither speak for a moment. The cub takes little bites of his sandwich.

"You know, it was hard for me when you met my mom."

"I know," the polar bear says.

"I didn't like you."

The polar bear grins. "Oh, I know."

"But Mom stopped crying."

"She used to cry?"

The cub peels back more plastic from the sandwich and takes another bite.

"After my dad left, she cried all the time. I was only little and I don't remember him much but I remember her crying." He finishes the sandwich and rolls the plastic into a small ball. "And now all she does is smile and laugh."

"Well, that's good," the polar bear says.

"So how can I not like you?"

The polar bear beams. "What's not to like?"

The cub grins back. "And all that crap at school—it's not because of you."

"I hope not."

"It's a new school and a new neighbourhood," the cub says. "It's different from where I came from. I'm the only black bear in the whole school. You don't know how hard that is."

The polar bear shrugs.

"You got me there. But your mom, she worries about you."

"Yeah, I know."

"We can talk about school later," the polar bear says. "But right now, me and you—we cool?"

"Yeah, we cool."

"Why you smiling?"

"Nothing," the cub says. "You're trying to talk like a black bear."

"What? I'm not cool enough for that?"

"Hell no," the cub says, and they both chuckle.

They sit a minute in silence, before the polar bear sits up.

"Look."

The cub peers across the room.

The polar bear nods to the far end of the room, toward the partition. There is a tuft of hair. The cub reaches for his rifle. The polar bear, still looking across the room, places his hand gently on the cub's rifle.

"Patience," he whispers.

They hold their stare to the far end of the room, over the cubicles and to the corner. The polar bear moves so that he is huddled up against the cub.

"Steady," he whispers. "You want it right in the middle of the chest, up high."

The cub turns his body so that he is lying flat, the rifle held tight.

"Keep the stock to your shoulder," the polar bear says.

The cub grips the gun tighter.

"Relax," the polar bear whispers.

The cub places his claw on the trigger. He breathes fast. The rifle shakes.

"Breathe," the polar bear whispers.

The cub breathes and the polar bear leans in closer still. "Good, good, just like that."

The cub's snout rests against the rifle, his head rests on the stock. The man is standing up straight now and the cub can see him clearly through the scope. He has him dead center.

"Breathe," the polar bear whispers again. "Inhale, exhale. Squeeze the trigger on the exhale. Don't do it till you're sure of the shot. Don't be in a hurry."

The cub blinks and readjusts himself then takes a breath. The rifle moves up and down with his breathing.

"When you've got him, squeeze on the exhale," the polar bear whispers.

The cub's snout rests along the stock. His heart beats fast in his chest. He breathes, timing his breath and steadying it so that he is in-between breaths when he squeezes the trigger. The rifle cracks and kicks hard into his shoulder and it all happens so fast he does not see the target drop.

"Whoooeee!" the polar bear cries, jumping up. "Dead center!" He grabs the rifle from the cub, clicks on the safety and steps out from behind the cabinet. "Hurry up. We don't have much time."

They rush across the room and find the man lying face-down. The polar bear kneels next to him and rolls him over. The cub stands back.

"Don't be afraid," the polar bear says. "He's dead. He's not gonna hurt you." He claws the shirt off the man's chest and spots the bullet hole. "Look at that—straight to the heart. What a shot! You're a natural." He rolls the body onto its side. "Come here, get down here."

The cub steps around the body and kneels.

"Hold the head up," the polar bear says.

The cub kneels and holds the head so that the face is upward, unnaturally perched, eyes open and blank, mouth agape. The polar bear hands the rifle to the cub and perches it against the body. The polar bear steps back and pulls out his phone.

"Say *honey!*"

The polar bear takes several quick photos and then reaches into his bag for a handsaw.

The cub frowns. "What's that for?"

The polar bear looks down at the bulk of the body and huffs.

"You think we're gonna lug this thing all the way back to the car? We take the head and as much meat as we can carry."

"The head?"

"I know a taxidermist who'll make him look as alive as he was a minute ago."

"Mom won't let me keep it. No way."

"I'll talk to her."

The cub's face brightens. "Put it in my room?"

The polar bear grins. "Don't push it. But maybe the garage."

The cub nods.

"Ok then," the polar bear says, kneeling. He places the blade of the saw against the neck. "Reach into my pack and grab the plastic bags. We got some work to do and we gotta get moving."

—4—

"Aim higher," the moose says. "You got a cross-wind there too. Look at the treetops. Looks like it's coming from the east. Put yourself a couple degrees to the right. You gotta account for the hill too, not just the wind. Or you wanna move closer? We can do that. Nobody will know."

The fawn stays steady. "No," he says. "I got it."

"Ok," the moose says. "Hold on a sec." He turns behind him, to the porcupine who is crouching off to the side, camera focused on Mel, with the moose and the fawn in the foreground.

"You can see him right there," the moose says into the camera. "He's nearly done. Just need the kill shot now."

The fawn stands, eyeing Mel. He raises the bow a little, then he releases it and the arrow whooshes through the air and lands with a thud into the ground a few feet in front of Mel.

The moose turns to the camera.

"It don't get no better than that!"

The porcupine lowers the camera and speaks low.

"He missed."

"Shut up," the moose says.

They make their way up the hillside. Mel is already dead.

The moose fires an arrow into his chest.

"Get in here," he says, as the porcupine moves in for a close shot. The moose is crouched. "Dead center! Man, can this kid shoot!" The phone buzzes in the pine needles and the moose crushes it under his hoof. He now sees the sweep of the river and the rolling hills beyond. "Look at this view. Make sure you get it."

The porcupine has already begun, panning the camera over the spread of the landscape.

The moose takes the body and sits it up, perching it upward so that the fawn can stand beside it with his bow. The moose steps in and kneels beside him and pats him on the back.

"For a midget you're pretty damned good, kid."

The porcupine sets up the shot, just as the panther appears from the brush.

"I got a ton of B-roll," the panther says. "Lots of good stuff."

"Go get the river again. You can't get enough of that," the moose says.

"I got lots."

"Get more," the moose says. "We got good daylight still. I don't wanna get back to the cutting room and you don't got enough shots."

The panther huffs and makes his way down the other side of the hill.

The moose grunts; he is posing now, chest inflated, his huge frame positioned straight to the porcupine's camera.

"All set?"

The porcupine nods. He has framed the shot so that the fawn, the moose, and the kill are right on the edge of the hill, with the long, winding sweep of the river far below.

"Beautiful," he says, looking through the camera. "Just beautiful."

The moose clears his throat.

"What a shot this young fella has. Unbelievable. All you kids out there watching, there ain't nothing you can't do if you put your mind to it." He pats the fawn on the shoulder. "Ain't that right, kid?"

The fawn smiles wide, his bow displayed proudly at his side.

The moose grins.

"Well, that concludes another successful hunt, and what a way to end the season. From all of us here on *The Bow Show*..." He turns to the fawn and they both look into the camera and say in unison: "Giddy up!"

The closet door bursts open. The target curls into a ball in the corner of the closet, shielding its face from the flashlight. The lion takes a step back and aims the rifle.

"Down a little," the rhino says. "Don't get the hair."

The lion lowers the rifle.

"Too low," the rhino says.

The lion raises the rifle.

The target's head is buried between its knees.

"Higher," the rhino says. "You ain't gonna kill it in the foot."

The lion holds the rifle.

"Go on," the rhino says. "Whatcha waiting for?"

The lion sighs, lowers the rifle then raises it again. A trickle of sweat drops into his eye and he blinks it away.

"Jesus," the rhino says. "Hurry up."

The target is crying. Whimpering.

The lion lowers the rifle.

"I can't."

The rhino huffs, points his rifle and fires two quick shots that plunk into the target's body, killing it instantly.

"For a lion, you're a real pussy, you know that?" He plops his backpack on the floor and pulls out a handsaw. "Gimme a hand here. If you're gonna get paid you can't just stand there and do nothing."

The lion is in a daze as the rhino grabs the body by the feet and drags it out of the closet and lays it flat on the bedroom floor.

"You're in charge of toenails," the rhino says. "I'll get the head. Now hurry up." He takes the lush blonde hair and props up the head. "Nice. Thick. Clean. Good cash for this." He looks up at the lion who is still standing by the closet. "We gotta hurry the hell up and get outta here. You hear me? Toenails!"

The lion nods.

"Don't break them," the rhino says. "They're only worth money whole. Get a good grip with the pliers and pull them straight out. Don't wiggle or go up or down. Straight out. Something to do with how they grind them up."

"Grind them up?"

"Yeah," the rhino says. "Put it in tea or some shit like that. Makes your pecker hard." He laughs. "I don't give a damn what it does—it's straight cash for us."

"Cash," the lion says flatly.

"Yeah, cash," the rhino says. "Which is why we're here. Stay focused."

The lion nods, half to himself.

The rhino places a plastic bag over the head and then stretches an elastic tightly around the neck. He sets the saw's blade to the neck and thrusts forward, cutting through the soft tissue and through the scrunch of bone. After a few thrusts the head is severed and he places it into another plastic bag. He grabs another pair of pliers and starts plucking the fingernails one at a time. He is quick and efficient and soon all ten fingernails, bloodied with bits of torn flesh, are in a small pile on the carpet.

The lion is still standing with the pliers. He stares down at the bag with the severed head, and the pool of blood, soaking into the carpet. There is blood everywhere. He places his paw over his mouth and heaves but does not vomit. He'd never been against hunting, but he was not prepared for this. No, he wasn't against it any more than he was against his wife's cherished vodka martinis, though the thought of both made him nauseous. But he thought he could do this for her; that he could swallow it and bury it down deep just this once. For her. And for his father too, but now, in the thick of it, he knew that would never happen; his father would be ashamed of him. This is not hunting and you are not a hunter, he says to himself. You're a poacher. All the codes—whatever they are—have been broken.

"Outta the way," the rhino says, shoving the lion aside. He kneels and plucks the toenails, dropping each one onto the fingernails. They sound like tiny seashells as they drop. He stands up and swats the lion on the leg and tosses a baggie at him, which falls to the floor. "Gather up those nails."

The lion looks at the rhino, stunned. Stunned from the heartlessness of it; that the rhino, whom he has known his whole life, is capable of this, and without a care in the world.

The rhino stares at the lion for a moment, then sighs and picks up the baggie and scoops up the nails and shoves it into his pocket. Then he stuffs the big bag into his backpack.

"Let's go."

Soon they are down the stairs and outside. It is a warm, clear night and the crickets are loud. The lion swats a mosquito from his face then starts across the courtyard to the far side of the barn, the way they'd come. He is relieved to be out of the house, out of that room of horrors.

The rhino stops abruptly. "Where you going?"

The lion turns. "Aren't we going home?"

The rhino shakes his head and grins wickedly.

"Not yet. There's more — probably young ones — worth twice as much."

The lion's heart drops into his gut with a thud. He can see, in the blue of the moonlight, the thin, newly broken trail in the hay leading down the field to the edge of the forest.

THE END